"I've got him." Joshua hurried toward her and took the baby carrier from her.

Sunlight glinted off something in the parking garage across the street. He took a closer look and saw the protruding piece of metal. The sight produced a distinctly bad feeling in his gut.

"Kaylee, go back inside."

"What? Why?"

A crack sounded, and the concrete spit shards up around the bottom of his calves.

Joshua simply moved, keeping himself between Duncan and the shooter in the parking garage. He rounded the front of the vehicle and had almost reached her when the glass door behind her shattered.

Silence reigned for a split second before screams echoed around him. With a tight grip on the handle of the carrier, Joshua grabbed Kaylee and shoved her through the door that no longer existed.

They made it inside just as the second bullet took out the glass of the other door.

Lynette Eason is a bestselling, award-winning author who makes her home in South Carolina with her husband and two teenage children. She enjoys traveling, spending time with her family and teaching at various writing conferences around the country. She is a member of Romance Writers of America and American Christian Fiction Writers. Lynette can often be found online interacting with her readers. You can find her at Facebook.com/lynette.eason and on Twitter, @lynetteeason.

Books by Lynette Eason

Love Inspired Suspense

Wrangler's Corner

The Lawman Returns
Rodeo Rescuer
Protecting Her Daughter
Classified Christmas Mission
Vanished in the Night

Classified K-9 Unit

Bounty Hunter

Rookie K-9 Unit

Honor and Defend

Capitol K-9 Unit

Trail of Evidence

Family Reunions

Hide and Seek
Christmas Cover-Up
Her Stolen Past

Visit the Author Profile page at Harlequin.com for more titles.

VANISHED
IN THE NIGHT

LYNETTE EASON

HARLEQUIN® LOVE INSPIRED® SUSPENSE

Recycling programs
for this product may
not exist in your area.

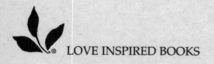 LOVE INSPIRED BOOKS

ISBN-13: 978-1-335-49041-4

Vanished in the Night

Copyright © 2018 by Lynette Eason

All rights reserved. Except for use in any review, the reproduction
or utilization of this work in whole or in part in any form by any
electronic, mechanical or other means, now known or hereafter
invented, including xerography, photocopying and recording, or in
any information storage or retrieval system, is forbidden without
the written permission of the editorial office, Love Inspired Books,
195 Broadway, New York, NY 10007 U.S.A.

This is a work of fiction. Names, characters, places and incidents are
either the product of the author's imagination or are used fictitiously, and
any resemblance to actual persons, living or dead, business establishments,
events or locales is entirely coincidental.

This edition published by arrangement with Love Inspired Books.

® and TM are trademarks of Love Inspired Books, used under license.
Trademarks indicated with ® are registered in the United States Patent
and Trademark Office, the Canadian Intellectual Property Office and in
other countries.

www.Harlequin.com

Printed in U.S.A.

Trust in the Lord with all thine heart;
and lean not unto thine own understanding. In all
thy ways acknowledge Him, and He shall direct thy paths.
—Proverbs 3:5-6

Dedicated to my family. I love you more.

ONE

Joshua Crawford gripped the steering wheel and hoped he could keep his cool when he confronted his mother about her lousy idea to marry the town drunk. "Hoped" being the key word. He drove with precise, automatic movements, each mile taking him closer to home and to the woman who'd loved and raised him and taught him right from wrong.

Which was why he was not going to allow her to throw the rest of her good years away on a man who could take advantage of a widow. Because that was just plain wrong. Of all the people—no, of all the unmarried people—in Wrangler's Corner, she'd picked Garrett Martin?

Joshua was actually worried about her mental state. No matter that she insisted the man was changed and treated her like a "precious jewel." Her words. Nope, not his mother. No way. His deceased father may have been best friends with the man, but that didn't mean his mother had to marry him.

As Joshua rounded the next curve that would take him into Wrangler's Corner, he slammed on the brakes. Rubber screeched on asphalt but his SUV responded well.

A black van sat in the middle of the street, blocking

both lanes, its hazard lights flashing. A wreck? Was anyone hurt? His hand went to the door handle.

At the sound of a woman's scream, he bolted out of the SUV and ran toward the black van. Only to skid to a stop. It was one inch from being T-boned up against the front of a light gray sedan.

A blond-headed woman struggled against a man's grip.

"Hey!" Joshua started toward them.

The man spun, freeing the woman who dropped to her knees and clutched her very pregnant belly. Her tent-like dress billowed around her as tears dripped down her cheeks. He met her attacker's gaze. "Get away from her. I'm calling the cops."

Joshua pulled his phone from his pocket and dialed 9-1-1. The man cursed, raced at Joshua and threw a right hook. If it had connected, it would have hurt, but Joshua easily deflected the intended blow.

With expert precision, he flipped the man, who landed on his back, gasping and blinking. The attacker rolled to his stomach, still trying to draw breath. Joshua started toward him to move him out of reach of the woman and found himself staring at the muzzle of a black pistol.

Joshua held his hands up and stepped back slightly. Even his extreme skills were no match for a bullet. "Whoa. There's no need for that."

The man rolled to his feet, keeping the weapon trained on Joshua. The woman let out another low cry, but Joshua couldn't do anything to help her. Not yet. His adrenaline spiked in a way he'd never felt before. "Get in your van and drive away," Joshua said.

"She's coming with me."

Joshua glanced at the puddle of water on the ground

at the woman's feet. "Actually, I think she's getting ready to have a baby. Have you ever delivered one?"

Before the attacker could respond, a blue truck approached and slowed. The older man behind the wheel lowered his window, his brow furrowed in concern. "Hey, y'all need any help?"

"No, we're fine, thanks," Joshua said. "It was a close call, but no one's hurt." He sure didn't want to involve an innocent bystander. From his position, the newcomer couldn't see the weapon in the other man's hand. Joshua planned to keep it that way.

"All right, then." The driver gave a wave and sped off.

"The cops are on the way," Joshua said. "That man saw your vehicle. You shoot me or hurt her, you'll be found."

A low growl escaped the man as he backed toward his van, never moving his weapon from Joshua. "You'll regret interfering. I'll be back." He climbed in and slammed the door then peeled away as he headed toward the highway.

Joshua let out a low breath and rushed to the woman's side even as he barked orders to the dispatcher still on the phone. He gave her the make and model of the van and the direction it was headed, but couldn't get the plate. However, he was able to describe the gun. He turned his attention to the moaning woman. "What's your name?"

"Kaylee…Martin." She gasped. "Oh-hh, it hurts."

He froze for a split second. Kaylee Martin? As in the daughter of the man his mother planned to marry? Great. Just great. With a tight smile, he took her arm and led her to his SUV. "Get in the back. How far apart are your contractions?"

"I don't know. I haven't exactly had a chance to time them." She let out a low gasp and closed her eyes. He waited for the contraction to pass. She looked up. "I need to get to the hospital. I was on the way when he pulled in front of me. I barely managed to stop without hitting him."

"I don't think there's time to get to a hospital. I'm a doctor, let me help you."

"No. I want my doctor and my hospital. Please, drive me."

Joshua hesitated.

She gave another low groan and bent, clutching her belly, still standing on the side of the road next to his SUV.

"Breathe through it," he said. "As soon as this contraction stops, you need to get into the back of my truck and I'm going to deliver your baby. Your contractions are coming too fast to make it anywhere. Where's your husband? You want me to call him?"

The contraction passed and she gripped his hand. "My husband is dead—and I wouldn't call him if he weren't. Now. Take me to the hospital." She panted a bit then caught her breath. "Please. I can't have this baby on the side of the road. What if something goes wrong? What if—?"

"All right, we can try. Just promise me you'll holler if you have to push. Understand?"

"Yes, yes. I understand."

She made it into the back seat before the next contraction hit her. He talked her through it. "I've got to move your car out of the middle of the road, okay? I'll be right back, I promise."

"Okay. Okay. It's fine. I can do this."

The compassionate doctor inside him took over. "Of course you can, Kaylee. I'll be there to help."

"The keys are in the ignition," she whispered. "Hurry."

* * *

Kaylee watched him leave and breathed a prayer to the God she wasn't sure was even listening. But just in case he was... *I don't know why stuff like this happens to me, but, please, get me through it. Help me. Let my baby be all right, healthy, whole and fine...*

"I'm back."

"Drive. Please drive. Fast."

Still, he hesitated. "Kaylee, we're an hour away—"

"Get in and drive! Please."

Joshua sighed and climbed into the driver's seat. "All right, but I can guarantee you we're not going to make it." He cranked the big Suburban and pulled onto the road that would take them toward Nashville's hospital.

"We'll make it," she said. "We have to make it." After all she'd been through, delivering her baby on the side of the road would just be the proverbial straw that broke the camel's back. No, she could do this. She was strong. She'd survived marrying into a mafia family— unbeknownst to her at the time—then being thrown out of said mafia family when her husband's parents disowned him. She'd lived through visiting her spouse in prison, learning about his affair, then being tossed out of her home, pregnant and penniless, by the very man who'd promised to love her forever. She was a survivor. If she had to have her child on the moon, she would do it, and they were going to have a wonderful life together. Her baby deserved it.

"What were you doing driving yourself?" he asked just as another contraction hit.

She panted her way through it before responding. "Dad wasn't answering his phone. I called two other friends, and they didn't answer. I waited to see if one of them would call me back. Obviously, I waited too long.

I didn't want to spend the money on an ambulance—"
Another contraction hit and she couldn't get another word
out. Kaylee clenched her teeth and tried to breathe at
the same time. She really should have done the classes,
but—"Ah!"

"Breathe, Kaylee. Breathe through it."

"You breathe through it! I don't want to *breathe
through it*. I want it to *stop*!" Then the pressure was
just too much. "Oh, no. I have to push. I have to!"

"Don't push!" The SUV slammed to a stop and then
he was there with the back door open. He rested one
hand on her right ankle. "Look, let me help you."

"I don't know you. You can help me by getting me
to the hospital."

"Don't you recognize me?"

She blinked at him, trying to focus. "No." She'd been
in pain and fear for the last ten hours. Everything was
kind of blurry. And the pressure...

"I'm Joshua Crawford. *Dr.* Joshua Crawford."

Another wave of pain hit her even as she processed
his name. Joshua Crawford. Oh, no. Not the son of the
woman who planned to marry her father. The gold digger who'd sunk her claws into him.

She remembered Joshua now. And wished she didn't.
But she *had* heard that he was a doctor. Hadn't she?
Or was he some mixed martial arts fighter? The pain
eased, the pressure lessened. But she knew it would be
back. "I thought you were on the MMA circuit. When
did you become a doctor?"

"I became the doctor first. MMA was later. Or rather,
during."

"What?"

"Never mind. I'll explain later."

More indescribable pain hit her. She couldn't speak

for the next couple of minutes, but once the contraction passed she looked at him and nodded. "Okay. Just make it stop." At least she had a doctor to help, so maybe God *did* care about her just a little. At the moment she didn't care, she was just thankful.

"Don't push."

"If you tell me not to push one more time—"

Joshua ran to the back of the SUV. In the midst of the contractions that seemed to come one after the other in a never-ending wave of pain, she heard him rummaging.

He returned and set a bag on the floor. "Try to relax. I've done this before."

"You've had a baby before?" She gritted the words. "I doubt it. If you had, you would never tell me to try to relax—or demand I not push."

He gave a low laugh. "No, I've never had a baby before, but I've delivered a few. Okay? How about try to take comfort in knowing that I'm going to take care of you and your little one?"

"That's better." She breathed through her mouth like she'd seen people do in the labor room where she'd worked a rotation. Surprisingly, it helped. A little.

"I don't have everything I would like, but I've got a large tarp and a medical bag. It'll have to do."

"I've got towels in my car. In case my water broke. I was sitting on them in the driver's seat."

"Okay, be right back."

He took off again and she did her best to breathe through the next contraction. When it was over, she sucked in a deep breath. "Whoa." She had a new appreciation for mothers who chose natural childbirth over having an epidural. She hadn't planned to do it this way.

She really wanted the epidural.

But it wasn't to be. Now she just wanted her baby here, whole and healthy.

Joshua returned, towels in hand.

"That was fast."

"I didn't have to go very far." He grinned. "I was driving really slow because I figured this was going to happen."

She'd take that up with him later.

"I'm ready when you are." He covered her with two of the towels and his respect for her privacy nearly made her cry. Then another wave of pain hit and she just plain didn't care anymore. She just wanted to be done. And to sleep. Yes. Sleep would be amazing.

"Fine. Just do it." She let out another yell and lost herself in the process of giving birth.

Kaylee wasn't aware of time passing. She was mostly aware of the pain, but also the excitement that the end was finally here. The end...and the beginning. The beginning of a new life *with* a new life.

And then Joshua was placing him in her arms and everything faded once more. Only this time there was no pain, just awe. She touched the baby's face. *Her* baby's face. And he was just perfect.

She looked up to find Joshua staring at her—at them. His eyes met hers. "Thank you," she whispered.

"You're welcome."

Joshua stripped his gloves from his hands and tossed them into a trash bag. He never traveled without his bag of medical supplies and, once again, it had paid off to have it.

He let his gaze travel the area, looking for the van used by Kaylee's attacker. While he'd been focused on delivering the baby, he couldn't help throwing glances over his shoulder every so often. He was almost surprised the man hadn't shown up. Grateful, but surprised.

For now, Kaylee and her baby were safe, and that was all that mattered. He glanced at her and found she was still enamored with the infant in her arms. Her son.

His heart thudded at how beautiful he found the sight. Her long, blond hair feathered around her face. She'd pushed some strands behind her right ear but they didn't want to stay there. Vivid blue eyes were now trained on her child, but Joshua remembered the fire in them when she'd tried to fight off her attacker and then again when she'd realized she was going to give birth in the back of his SUV. He drew in a deep breath. Beautiful or not, she was off-limits.

The ambulance had arrived five minutes after the baby boy had slid into his hands. Now the paramedics were waiting to take Kaylee and her son to the hospital to be checked out. His cousin, Sheriff Clay Starke, was also waiting. "Be with you in a minute."

"Sure."

Joshua approached the nearest paramedic, a blonde in her midthirties. "I think she's ready."

"Great." She and her partner, an older guy, grabbed the gurney and rolled it over to the SUV. They gently helped Kaylee and the baby out of the back seat and onto the gurney.

Joshua re-gloved, rolled up the soiled tarp and disposed of it in the ambulance's hazardous waste bag. He turned to find Clay talking to Kaylee. "...you know the man? Can you describe him?"

"No. I've never seen him before, I'm sorry. I..." She gave a small shrug and shook her head.

"Did he say what he wanted?"

"He wanted me to get in the van and, when I refused,

he grabbed my arm. That's when Joshua drove up and fought him off."

At Clay's raised brow, Joshua shrugged. "I did some mixed martial arts training to help deal with the stress of medical school. I picked up a few moves."

She met his gaze. "I've never seen anyone fight like that. You made it look so easy."

"At least until he pulled the gun, huh?" He could have disarmed the man with a few simple moves. And if Kaylee hadn't been standing in the path of a possible bullet, he would have.

"Well, yes, but still, that was pretty amazing."

He smiled. "I've had some practice."

She bit her lip. "Thank you for being there. I don't know what I would have done—with him or the baby." She blinked back tears and he thought one of the walls around his heart might have just cracked a little.

He cleared his throat and backed up a bit. "It was good timing."

Clay slapped him on the back. "Nice work. Glad to have you back home. Mom and Dad are looking forward to seeing you."

"I'm looking forward to seeing them, as well."

Clay turned to Kaylee. "Is there anyone we should call?"

"My father. I suppose."

"I'll call him now."

"Thanks."

"We're ready to roll." The paramedic shut the door.

"Should I follow her?" Joshua asked.

"Why?"

"Because whoever came after her just a bit ago isn't done. He said he'd be back."

And no matter who their parents were or the conflict that might wind up generating between him and Kaylee, he was worried her attacker might return—and he wasn't about to leave her and her son unprotected.

TWO

Kaylee woke slowly, her body sore, but her heart at peace—at least before her brain kicked in. Her gaze drifted to the white board opposite the bed and noted a new message written on it.

> Stopped in to see you, but you were sleeping. Didn't want to wake you. Call me when you're up to visitors—and when you're ready to move in. Xoxo, Nat.

Natalie Cross, her best friend in high school and the one person she trusted implicitly. Two weeks ago, she'd offered to let Kaylee move in with her, but as a lawyer with one of the most prestigious law firms in Nashville, she wasn't around much. While she had a home in Wrangler's Corner that had been in her family for several generations, she kept an apartment in the city for her late nights and early mornings.

Kaylee had yet to make up her mind, but she was leaning in that direction. She would have her own place and help her friend out by keeping up with the house. It might turn out to be a fabulous arrangement when she was ready to move out of her father's house. Which was going to be soon.

Especially if her father's marriage went through. She shifted to pick up the baby from his bassinet beside her bed and noticed the bruises her attacker had left on her upper right arm.

But she was safe.

And she had a beautiful baby boy, thanks to Dr. Joshua Crawford. A man who hadn't hesitated to help. So very different from most of the men she'd crossed paths with. Men like her dead husband. Or the man who'd stalked her until he'd finally made his move and tried to kidnap her.

The thought of her stalker sent her brain spinning back to the man who'd tried to grab her yesterday. If she hadn't gotten a good look at him, she would have believed her stalker had returned. But that was impossible. Thanks to the quick action of a neighbor, Patrick Talbot had been arrested the night he'd attempted to kidnap her and was now in custody awaiting trial.

Kaylee shuddered, not wanting to think about the man who'd made her life miserable for a little over six months. She still didn't know what it was she'd done that had focused his attention on her. But that had been over for weeks now, and she didn't have to worry or think about him again until it came time for her to testify. With a determined effort, she pushed him out of her mind and turned her thoughts to her father.

He'd been in for a visit and had seemed distant, quiet. He'd stood over the bassinet, looking down at the baby with one of the strangest expressions Kaylee had ever seen. Then he'd wished her well, excused himself and slipped out the door. She supposed she should be glad he'd at least come by.

With a mental shrug, she dismissed thoughts of her father and stroked the downy-soft cheek. "You need a name, don't you?"

She'd not wanted to know the gender of the baby before he was born. As a result, she'd decorated only a little after she'd moved in with her father. And while she'd had offers of help from Mrs. Crawford, she simply couldn't bring herself to accept it—or the fact that the woman would be marrying her father in three weeks.

Yes, her father was known for his drinking issues, but as far as she could tell, that was in the past, just as he claimed. Since she'd been living in his home, she hadn't seen a drop of alcohol in the place.

Of course, she didn't know what he did when he left the house.

But could it possibly be true?

Then again, he also had a lot of money from some smart real-estate investments, and while people judged him for his drinking—not everyone believed he'd quit— they sure didn't mind taking his money. Or marrying him to get it. Women tended to overlook his questionable past while trying to get their hands on his cash. However, he'd ignored them all.

Until Olivia Crawford.

Kaylee couldn't stop the tide of resentment. Toward both her father and his fiancée. Nor could she stop the guilt. She knew it wasn't right, but what was she to do about it? Pretend it wasn't there? Pray for God to change her heart? She probably should. After all, she'd known Mrs. Crawford practically all her life, and if the woman wasn't marrying her father, Kaylee would adore her. So, what was her *problem*? Why was she so out of sorts about this marriage?

Because she believed Mrs. Crawford had proved that

she was just like every other woman in town and out to grab her father's fortune. Then again, why did she care? If he was so blind, what did it matter to her? She sighed. Because he was still her father and she had a responsibility to look out for him even if he didn't return the sentiment. And, in a way, she felt like she should look out for Mrs. Crawford. Her father was no prize catch, that was for sure.

A knock on the door jerked her from her conflicted thoughts. "Come in."

The door swung open and Joshua stepped inside. Kaylee's heart stalled while he shut the door behind him. When he turned back, his warm blue eyes met hers. "Hi."

"Hi," she said. Her eyes dropped down when the baby stirred.

Joshua watched in awe as the little one's eyes opened and blinked at his mother. His mouth rounded into a small *O* before his lids dropped again. Joshua's heart filled with an emotion he couldn't name and wasn't sure he should examine too closely. In fact, he should push it far, far away. Hadn't he learned his lesson when it came to attractive women with children? "Don't get involved" had been his motto for the past two years. Why was he actually reconsidering that?

And then her focus was back on him. "What are you doing here?"

He tried to read if she was glad, angry or simply indifferent in the question, but he couldn't put his finger on it. "I hope it's all right. I just came to check in on you."

"Of course it's all right. But why?"

Heat surged into his cheeks and he shrugged, hoping

she wouldn't notice. "Because I wanted to make sure you and the baby were okay." He should have stayed away, but he simply hadn't been able to. He was over-reacting and being silly. It wasn't like he planned to marry the woman. He was just concerned.

Get a grip, Joshua.

"We're fine. In fact, we'll be leaving first thing to-morrow morning. You didn't have to come by."

Joshua sighed. She didn't want him there.

"But for some strange reason, I'm glad you did," she said softly.

His heart lifted in spite of the sermon he'd just preached to himself about staying uninvolved. "You are?"

"I am. I'm so grateful. If it wasn't for you, I would have given birth in the back of—" She swallowed and looked away. "Well, let's just say I'm grateful and leave it at that."

He took her hand, wondering if all of his preconceived notions about this woman were false. Had he judged her too quickly?

She shivered. "Why is your mother marrying my father?"

He paused. "So, you'll talk to me about it?"

"Of course I'll talk about it. If you'll help me stop it. Or at least figure it out."

He frowned. "Why do you want to stop it? My mother is a perfectly fine, upstanding lady."

"I sure thought she was. So, why would she agree to marry someone like my father? He doesn't exactly have the best reputation in town."

Her question threw him. "Ah... I don't know. I'll be sure to ask her when I see her." He didn't bother tell-ing that had been priority number one before he'd had to alter his plans to fight off her attacker and deliver her baby. He nodded to the infant. "What's his name?"

"I haven't decided."

He lifted a brow. "Well, you can't just keep calling him Baby. Or Bubba."

"Bubba?" A smile curved her lips. "I've not once referred to him as Bubba, I assure you."

Whoa. Her smile packed a punch. He cleared his throat. "What's wrong with Bubba?"

"Not a thing. Bubba is a perfectly respectable name for those who choose it. I'm just not calling my child that, so don't start."

He shrugged. "I'm kidding, of course. Why don't you have a name picked out, though? What about naming him after his father?"

She flinched and her eyes narrowed. "I wouldn't name him after his father if it were the only name left on the planet. I want my son to grow up to be good and honorable, to be a man who respects women and loves God. I'll name him after someone who deserves it."

Okay, then. There was a story behind those words.

Joshua eased into the chair beside her bed and held out his arms. "Sounds like things a good mother teaches her child. What did your husband do to make you so mad at him?"

She hesitated, then placed the baby in his arms. "He found someone else."

"Ouch." He knew the feeling. "Yes, that would do it."

"And then was killed while he was sleeping next to her."

He jerked and stared at her. "Seriously?"

"Seriously."

"Wow. Who killed him?"

"The woman's husband. He was found guilty of murder and is now serving a life sentence."

Okay, so he probably should stop feeling sorry for himself. She'd been through much worse than he. Joshua settled back into the chair and held the infant in the crook of his arm. "I'm afraid I have no idea what to say to that one."

A sigh slipped from her. "There's nothing to say." Silence fell between them and he adjusted the blanket over the tiny arm. "You're good at that," she said softly.

"I like babies."

And she liked the image of him holding her son way too much. She almost snatched the child from him, but instead, sighed and rubbed her eyes. When she opened them, she found Joshua staring at the baby with one of the most gentle, caring expressions she'd ever seen on a man.

"What's your name?"

He looked up, confusion in his eyes. "Joshua."

"I know that. I mean your full name."

"Joshua Duncan Crawford. But don't you dare call me JD."

"Why? You like Bubba better?"

He laughed.

She thought about it. "I like it. I think I'll call him Duncan."

"What? After me?"

She held his stunned gaze. "Why not? You've shown him more care and gentleness than anyone else in his short life. A life he still has because you intervened today. I can't think of anyone I'd rather name him after."

He opened his mouth then shut it. Opened it again. "What about your father?" he finally said.

She shook her head. "No."

"Are you sure?"

"I'm sure."

"Then I'm honored," he said softly. He lifted the baby and gazed into the sleeping face. "Nice to meet you, Duncan."

Kaylee thought she might burst into tears. His tenderness, his care…yes, Duncan was the perfect name for her son.

Joshua continued to talk to the newly named baby, and she let her eyes drift shut. Just for a moment. Then she'd take Duncan and feed him.

When she woke, the sun was down and the dark night snuggled up against the windowpane. The chair beside the bed was empty. She turned to check on Duncan and gasped at the empty bassinet.

In place of the baby, someone had left a white box. A box just like the one she'd received before she'd left her job in Nashville.

Terror struck. Her stalker was back. And he'd taken her son.

Kaylee threw the covers back and lowered her feet to the slippers someone had so kindly placed next to her bed. With trembling fingers, she snatched the robe from the end of the bed and tossed it around her shoulders.

She rushed to the door and threw it open—only to come to a halt. "Mrs. Crawford?"

The dark-haired woman turned from speaking with two of the nurses—with Duncan in her arms. Kaylee pressed a hand to her pounding heart and walked over to her. "What are you doing?"

"Oh, I worried you, didn't I? I'm so sorry." She immediately handed the baby to Kaylee, who gathered him close and inhaled his sweet scent. Her knees trembled and tears gathered at the back of her throat.

But Duncan was safe. Her stalker was in custody. He hadn't left the box. She could relax. The fact that she'd immediately reverted to her jumpy, nerve-racking, stalker days frustrated her. But that box...

The woman placed a hand on Kaylee's shoulder and squeezed. "You were sleeping so soundly, I hated to wake you. Joshua had to leave. Clay called him and asked him to come in to discuss the attack on you in more detail. As he was leaving, he introduced your little man to me. Then he started to fuss, so I picked him up and fed him his bottle."

"Oh. Well, thank you." Kaylee had needed the sleep, definitely felt better because of it, but the last thing she wanted was for this woman to form an attachment to her child.

But at least Mrs. Crawford wouldn't hurt him.

Kaylee chided herself for her initial fear. If anyone had taken her baby through the hospital doors, all kinds of alarms would have gone off.

She sighed. The day's events had rattled her more than she wanted to admit. "I'm going back to my room. Thank you for stopping by." She turned to go.

"Kaylee?"

Kaylee stopped. "Yes?"

"Could we talk for a few minutes?"

Mrs. Crawford was one of the last people she wanted to talk to, but she didn't want to be rude, either. "Sure."

Kaylee led the way into her room and sat on the bed.

The white box mocked her. Mrs. Crawford had probably left it there when she'd taken Duncan to feed him. The fact that the box was the same as the one from her stalker was just a coincidence. Kaylee's back stiffened.

She had no desire for gifts from the woman she considered a gold digger.

Mrs. Crawford took the chair her son had vacated sometime earlier. "We have a lot to talk about."

Kaylee pulled her gaze from the box. "Like what?"

"Well, for one—" Mrs. Crawford said, "—I know you adored your mother and I could never take her place. I wouldn't even try, but can we at least be friends?"

Taken aback, Kaylee sank her teeth into her bottom lower lip as she considered her response. "Mrs. Crawford, why did you agree to marry my father?" she finally asked.

Mrs. Crawford blinked. "First, please call me Olivia. And I agreed to marry your father because I love him."

Kaylee gaped. "But why? He's so totally unlovable." Except for his money, Kaylee truly couldn't see the draw to the man. "I'm his daughter, and I can hardly stand to be around him." And yet, he'd allowed her to move back into her old room and have one of the spares for the baby. Of course, that was a temporary arrangement, as she planned to move out as soon as it was feasible—especially if he was truly getting married again—but he'd let her.

Olivia crossed her legs. "How long have you been gone from Wrangler's Corner? It's been a few years, yes?"

"Four years. I left shortly after high school because I couldn't stand to be in the same town with him. He's overbearing, controlling, manipulative—"

"Yes, he was all those things—and he readily admits it."

Kaylee snapped her mouth shut. "Since when?" she finally managed.

"Since he got out of rehab and turned his life around."

The woman kept throwing bombshells at her. "Rehab? What rehab?"

"That's what I meant by we have a lot to talk about."

"I've been home for two weeks and I haven't seen any indication that he's a changed man—except I haven't seen any alcohol in the house." And he hadn't completely avoided her. But she hadn't really given him the opportunity to prove that he'd changed. She simply left the room whenever he entered.

"That's one indication then, isn't it?"

Kaylee gave a grudging nod. "He came to the hospital and didn't even hold Duncan."

But she had to admit, her father hadn't yelled at her once since she'd been back.

Olivia frowned. "It's probably just because he's unsure and nervous."

Kaylee laughed. "He hasn't been unsure or nervous a day in his life."

"Not when he was drinking. The alcohol gave him some kind of a false bravado, but now...give him a chance, honey. Give *us* a chance. We just want to be here and love you and Duncan. Please?"

"I would actually love to believe that's true, but—" She cleared her throat of the sudden lump that had formed. "I guess the best I can do is to try and reserve judgment. For now."

Olivia nodded. "All right. We'll take that. For now." She reached into her bag and pulled out a small box. "It's not much, but this is for Duncan."

Kaylee frowned. Another gift? "But didn't you leave that box?" She pointed to the one in Duncan's bassinet.

Olivia frowned. "No. Why?"

A tremor ripped through Kaylee. She forced herself to breathe. "Okay, if you didn't, then who did?"

"I don't know, hon. It wasn't there when I came in to see you—and when I picked up Duncan."

Kaylee felt sick. Her first instinct had been right. Maybe.

"Do you want me to hold Duncan while you open it?" Olivia asked.

"No." Kaylee forced a smile. "It's all right. Someone must have popped in while I was sleeping and left it." Natalie, maybe? Maybe, but the box reminded her of previous "gifts." And Natalie had already given her a gift.

"All right," Olivia said. "I'll see you later." She rose, walked to the door, gave Kaylee one last smile and slipped out.

Kaylee leaned her head back against the pillow and let a few tears slip out. What was she going to do? Olivia Crawford was a very nice woman. At least, that was the way she came across. So, she was either a very good actress or she sincerely meant every word she said.

Time would tell.

She swallowed and looked at the box again. Telling herself she was being silly, that one of her father's friends or Natalie had left it, she held Duncan in the crook of her right arm and, using a fingernail on her left hand, lifted the lid to the pretty white box. She slipped it off and stared at the gift.

A dozen black roses stared back at her.

THREE

Joshua paced his mother's den and raked a hand through his hair. "How can you do this? Don't you know his reputation?" He'd had to wait on her for two hours before she'd come home only to zip in, change clothes, kiss his cheek and head back out. He'd given up and gone to bed at eleven thirty. She'd come home sometime after midnight.

This morning, he refused to let her out the door without confronting her. "Just tell me. Please."

"I'm not blind or deaf. Of course I know his reputation. But it's in his past. He's not the same person he was two years ago."

"So you keep saying." He heard the sarcasm in his voice and couldn't do anything about it.

She stood. "Yes. He's changed. You don't think people can change?"

"People like Garrett Martin? No. No, I don't."

"Then you need to spend some time in prayer. You can go to your room now."

Joshua's jaw dropped. "What?"

"You heard me. I'm a grown woman. I can make my own decisions about who I will and will not marry."

"And I'm a grown man. You can't send me to my room."

"My house, my rules. Just like it's always been." She stared at him. He stared back.

And finally dropped his eyes. "Mom, I don't want to fight with you." And he wouldn't disrespect her. "All right, tell me. What is it about him that you love so much?"

She sighed. "We've been friends for a long time. He and your father were friends as well, you know that. Garrett Martin is a good man. Deep down. He loved Stella so much. When she died, it nearly killed him. He pulled away from everyone, including poor Kaylee, and poured himself into his work."

"And poured alcohol down his throat."

"Not to the extent that everyone thinks. Yes, he got a DUI shortly after Stella's funeral. And yes, four years ago, the pastor found him passed out in the back pew of the church. Garrett was mortified and it was his wake-up call. Pastor Hall got him into a six-month rehab program. Your father and I visited and supported him. Encouraged him. When he got out, he wrote a long letter about how much our friendship meant to him. And then your father died, and Garrett was there for me."

"I remember him at the funeral."

"Yes."

"I'm just having a hard time wrapping my mind around this. Kaylee is, too. I guess I just don't understand how it happened."

She smiled. "It happens for older people the same way it does you young people. The late-night chats, after-work dinners and Sunday-morning worship services have all led to something more. Something special. He needed someone and I was there as a friend.

When I needed a friend, he was there. And now…it's just more."

"He needed someone, huh?"

"Yes, he did."

"And that someone had to be you?"

She tiled her head and studied him. "No, it didn't. It could have been anyone, but I chose for it to be me."

"Mom—"

"Drop it."

"I'm not dropping it. Not by a long shot." He paused. "What about Kaylee? Garrett pushed her away to the point she may never want anything to do with him again."

Sadness flickered. A real grief that shot pangs through him. "I know. That's Garrett's one remaining relationship he wants to repair, but is so unsure how to go about it."

"I don't know how to help there. Kaylee only returned home because she was desperate and alone."

"I know, but the fact that she was willing to move in with him gives him hope that this will provide them another chance to get to know one another and allow him to make up for his neglect as a father."

"I really hope it works out. If not for him, then for Kaylee. I think she needs him."

"Of course she does. He needs her, as well. Anytime there's discord or conflict between a parent and their child, it causes that parent severe inner turmoil." She raised a brow at him.

He met her gaze. "I'm sure it does the same to the child." With a glance at his watch, he sighed. "I have to go. Clay texted and said he was going to go by and talk to Kaylee before she's discharged from the hospital. He asked me to be there."

"You?"

"Well, I did fight off the guy that attacked her."

"I know." She frowned. "You could have been shot."

"But I wasn't." He grabbed his keys from the end table then kissed her cheek. "I love you. We'll talk later."

"Talk or argue?" she called after him.

"Probably both." He climbed into the SUV, slammed the door and started the vehicle.

The hour's drive to the hospital passed quickly for him and he soon found himself on Kaylee's floor. Her door was open and he could hear Clay's voice coming from inside the room.

"You didn't think you needed to tell anyone that you had a stalker?"

"No. I mean, I thought it was all done. He's in custody. How could it be him?" Kaylee said.

Joshua stepped into the room. "What's this about a stalker?"

"Kaylee had one back in Nashville," Clay said. "Looks like he's returned to finish the job."

"Finish what job?"

Clay read from a piece of paper in his gloved hand. "'You thought I was gone, but I'm not. I would never abandon you. I've had a lot of time to plan it all out. I know we can be very happy. I know you think you don't want to be with me, but I'll show you how much you can love me—and how much I love you. I hope you like the black roses. Red roses are so cliché, so I decided to be different. Different just like our life together will be. We have so much to look forward to. See you soon, my darling.'"

Kaylee held the baby against her shoulder. She'd read the words and had debated what to do. If Patrick Talbot wasn't sitting in jail, she would have no doubt who could have sent the "gift." She supposed he could have had someone, like his brother, do it for him, but as far as she knew, Patrick's family didn't have a lot to do with him. At least, that had been her understanding. She'd spoken to his brother and sister and they'd been severely grieved at his actions. Stalking with letters, then escalating to breaking into her home and trying to take her. If not for the quick actions of her neighbor, Kaylee wasn't sure how that would have ended. Although, she had a pretty good idea. She shuddered.

After opening the box, she'd left three messages with the detective who'd handled the case and he still hadn't returned her calls. Then she'd tried Patrick's lawyer and he hadn't answered, either. Her last call had been at three o'clock this morning when she'd finally contacted Clay Starke and explained the situation. The sheriff had arranged protection on her room for the remainder of the night and promised to be at the hospital first thing this morning. She'd been waiting for him when he'd walked in.

"What's the story behind this?" Joshua asked. "Catch me up."

Clay nodded and Kaylee sighed. "I had a stalker," she said. "Three months ago, he broke into my home and tried to kidnap me. He is currently in custody and awaiting trial. He was a former ER patient—one of those in-and-out kind of things. I didn't remember him until the detectives put it together during the investigation. I don't know why he focused on me. Before he was caught, I thought the gifts and notes and were from a different patient but—"

"Wait a minute," Joshua said. "You keep talking about patients? What's your occupation?"

"I'm a trauma nurse." She gave a half-hearted laugh.

"You'd never know it by the way I freaked out giving birth, but I'm actually a good nurse. I now work at the Wrangler's Corner clinic in town with Dr. Anderson."

Joshua smiled. "You didn't freak out, you were just in a new situation and needed a little help."

"You're kind."

Clay shot Joshua a look that said, "Be quiet." He turned back to Kaylee. "Go on. Why would you think it was this other patient?"

"He'd been involved in a hit-and-run by a drunk driver. His wife and unborn child were killed and he was hurt pretty badly. But he lived and was soon transferred out of ICU to a floor. I visited him occasionally just to check on him. He was there for two months while he recovered and I seemed to be the only one he responded positively to. He was grieving his wife, the loss of his baby…" She shrugged. "I would talk to him. Encourage him. Hold his hand while he wept. I told him about my own failed marriage and how my husband had deserted me and the baby. It made him angry on my behalf."

Kaylee rubbed her eyes. "I cared about him. I wanted to help him. And he says I did. That my visits kept him sane." She shook her head. "In the end, the police investigated him and it wasn't him. A neighbor saw Patrick Talbot break into my house and called the cops. They arrived as he was trying to drag me out of my house to his car." She swallowed. "He ran, but they caught him. I was stunned. Like I said, he'd been a patient in the ER." She held her hands up in a helpless gesture. "So many patients come through that ER, I can't remember them all."

"Of course not," Clay said.

"Did he say why he targeted you?" Joshua asked.

"No." She frowned. "Not really."

"So, the guy that tried to grab you in the street yesterday," Joshua said. "No idea who that was?"

"No. I've never seen him before."

Joshua frowned.

"What about the baby's father?" Clay asked. "Would he come after the baby?"

"He's dead," Kaylee said. "He was killed about a month after I told him I was pregnant. And he kicked me out when I told him. Trust me, even if he was alive, he would be the last one to come after me."

Clay frowned, compassion in his eyes. He nodded. "All right. I'll look into this stalker of yours. Patrick Talbot, right?"

"Yes. I tried calling the detective who handled the case, but he's not answering or calling me back. And I tried calling Patrick's lawyer, but again, no answer or call back."

Clay made a note of the names and their numbers. "I'll get these flowers to the lab in Nashville and have them see if they can pull any prints." He walked into the bathroom, came back with one of the bath towels and wrapped the box in it. "Did you touch the box?"

"I lifted the top with my fingernail." She shivered. "Once I realized what was in there, I didn't touch anything else. The note was sitting on top, so it was easy to read." A wave of nausea hit her. When would the drama stop? She was tired of everything, the constant emotional roller coaster, the daily battle life had become.

"Where did you live after your husband kicked you out of your home?" Joshua asked. "That's a big gap of time between then and now."

"I stayed with my sister-in-law, Marla, and her husband for about two weeks, but it was just too awkward.

In spite of being told I was welcome to stay, I moved in with a friend and fellow coworker from the hospital. Since the justice system moves so slow, and there's no telling when Patrick's trial will be, I decided to come back to Wrangler's Corner. Even though I had some good friends and support there, I just couldn't handle being in Nashville anymore."

"I understand." Clay tapped his notebook against his chin then nodded. "All right, I'm going to look into all of this and see what I can find out. In the meantime, be careful and take care of your little one."

She nodded. Clay picked up the towel-wrapped box and left, his phone already pressed to his ear.

Joshua took Duncan from Kaylee and cuddled him against his chest. "He's a cute little thing."

"Yes, he's a sweetheart."

"You need a ride home?"

She bit her lip and glanced at her cell phone on the table. She'd left a message for her father, but he'd not returned her call. He was probably at the office and not paying attention to his phone. "I guess so." She gasped. "I left the car seat in my car."

"I know. I saw it yesterday and grabbed it a little while ago on my way over here. It's in the back of my SUV—and I had your car towed to your father's house."

She stared. "Really? That was incredibly thoughtful. Thank you."

He shrugged. "You're welcome."

Kaylee couldn't believe how this man kept coming to her rescue. "Have you talked to your mother about her decision to marry my father?"

"I have. A little."

"And?"

"Let's just say, we're running out of time."

* * *

Running out of time. Yes, that was an apt description. He had slightly less than three weeks to talk his mother out of her crazy plan to marry Kaylee's father—and to keep Kaylee and little Duncan safe from the stalker before he had to return to Nashville. He hadn't saved them both just to let them fall prey to a crazy man.

With Kaylee at his side, Joshua carried the baby in the car seat, the handle fitting comfortably in his grip. Kaylee had dressed in a pair of loose, linen pants and a long, light blue T-shirt that brought out her eyes. Eyes he felt he would enjoy seeing on a daily basis.

The thought made him pause.

"What's wrong?" Kaylee was looking at him with those blue eyes.

He cleared his throat. "Ah, nothing. The elevator's at the end of this hall."

She nodded and walked ahead of him and yet, he still pictured her face. Her beautiful eyes, slightly turned up nose and that dimple in her left cheek.

He didn't need to notice any of that. He was there to watch over her and Duncan. Period.

Kaylee pressed the Down button then leaned over Duncan to make sure his little blue blanket was tucked around his chin. He yawned and settled back into sleep.

"When did you start working at the clinic in town?" Joshua asked.

"The second day I was here." She smiled at him. "When I got here, I had a horrible sinus infection. I walked in and Doc Anderson was there. I couldn't believe he was still working. When I asked him about retiring, he said he hadn't found the person he could entrust his practice to yet." She shrugged. "Anyway, I asked him if he needed a nurse and he hired me on the spot even though I was practically ready to give birth."

"He's a good man."

"And a fabulous doctor. He might be old, but he stays up-to-date on all the latest in the medical field."

The elevator arrived and she stepped inside. Joshua followed her and set the baby carrier on the floor. The doors closed and the car moved, taking them down.

Joshua rubbed a hand through his hair. "Mom said something about a doctor shortage in Wrangler's Corner."

"A human doctor shortage. There's no lack of veterinarians, that's for sure."

"That's because there are more animals than people in town."

"True."

"What made you try to make it to the hospital instead of letting Doc Anderson deliver Duncan?"

She grimaced. "He was about an hour away helping one of the Amish men in Ethridge. He'd fallen from the roof of his barn. Trust me, that man needed the doc more than I did—at least I thought so." She shot him a warm glance. "Fortunately, you came along when you did."

Her look seared him, made him want to wrap her and Duncan in Bubble Wrap and keep them locked safely behind closed doors.

He gave a silent snort. Now he sounded like a crazy stalker. Only, his intentions were good.

When the elevator opened, they stepped into the lobby. A large welcome area dominated the space with a desk and security guard leaned against it talking to two women.

"Wait here inside and I'll bring the truck around."

She nodded and he set the baby next to her. He hated

to leave her alone, but the security guard was right there. She should be fine for the few minutes it would take him to pull the SUV around to the circle—and it was better than having her walk out in the open to the parking garage.

He jogged to the garage and took the elevator to the third floor. When he stepped off, he caught sight of the back of a man who came from the stairs. A woman to his right was pulling a child from the back seat of her minivan. Other than that, the place was quiet. Empty.

Chills skittered up his arms, raising the hair there. *You'll regret interfering. I'll be back.* Kalyee's attacker's words rang in his ears. Was that man her stalker? No, not possible. Patrick Talbot was in jail.

So, who was the guy who'd tried to snatch her in the middle of the road? Joshua shook his head and picked up the pace. He'd said he'd be back. Would he be watching the hospital? Surely, he knew this was where they would be. If he wanted to find her, it wouldn't be hard—as the box of black roses testified.

Joshua's SUV was parked on the end in the second row. He glanced around and noted the security cameras. Nah. No one would try anything that could be caught on video, right?

Then again, some people didn't care. The attacker who'd tried to nab a pregnant woman in broad daylight hadn't worried about being seen or stopped. And he'd been ready to kill if it suited him. Joshua wasn't sure, but he had a feeling the guy hadn't pulled the trigger because of the man who'd stopped to ask if they'd needed help. Whatever had made him decide to run instead of shoot, Joshua didn't know and didn't really care. He was just glad it had ended the way it had. Then again, he had a feeling it wasn't over, either. And the guy *had* said he'd be back.

Joshua climbed into the SUV and cranked the engine. The low purr never failed to bring him satisfaction. His phone buzzed and he pulled it from the clip on his belt. Clay. "Yeah?"

"Patrick Talbot is out."

"Out? How?"

"He had a fancy lawyer who managed to find a loophole in the arrest. He was released a week ago."

"And no one called to tell Kaylee?"

"The detective said he tried, but apparently she changed her number and never gave him the new one. He said he'd just gotten her messages and was getting ready to call her when I rang."

"Great. That's just great," Joshua muttered.

"I know."

"All right. I'm getting ready to take her and the baby to her father's house. Want to meet us there?"

"I'd feel better if you had an escort. Stay there and let me see if I can get someone to follow you to Wrangler's Corner."

"I'll let her know."

He disconnected and drove around to the front entrance to the hospital. Pulling up to the door, he could see Kaylee standing at the glass window waiting for him. His heart did that funny little dance it seemed to want to do whenever he was in her presence.

Telling himself to get over it—that she was as off-limits to him as his mother was to her father—he parked and climbed out of the SUV. He had to ignore the little voice reminding him that his mother was engaged to that off-limits man. He grunted. Being attracted to

Kaylee was one thing, acting on it was another. Right now she needed a protector, not a Romeo.

Kaylee opened the hospital door, her bag slung over her shoulder and the baby carrier gripped in her other hand. She walked toward the SUV.

Joshua hurried to her. "I've got him." He took the carrier from her. For a little bitty thing, lugging him around in his seat required some muscles. Joshua rounded the front of the vehicle and opened the back door where he'd placed the base of the baby's safety seat.

Sunlight glinted off something in the parking garage across the street. A sharp flicker of light that made him squint. He took a closer look and saw the protruding piece of metal. The sight produced a distinctly bad feeling in his gut.

I'll be back.

"Kaylee, go back inside."

"What? Why?"

A crack sounded and the concrete spit shards up around the bottom of his calves.

Joshua simply moved, keeping Duncan's carrier in front of him and out of sight of the shooter. He rounded the front of the vehicle and had almost reached Kaylee when the glass door behind her shattered.

Silence reigned for a split second before screams echoed around him. With a tight grip on the handle of the carrier, Joshua grabbed Kaylee and shoved her through the door that no longer existed.

They made it inside just as the second bullet took out the glass of the other door.

FOUR

Kaylee huddled over her baby, tucking his carrier against her midsection while Joshua wrapped his arms around her. His chest pressed into her back and all she could think was that he was going to die because of her.

Another shot pinged off the tile floor and she flinched. Hospital security burst onto the scene. The security guard and one other officer who must have already been in the building raced into the lobby, weapons drawn.

"Everyone stay down!"

Really? They thought they had to say that? A hysterical giggle threatened to slip out and Kaylee swallowed hard. She had to keep it together. Her baby needed her. Sirens screamed in the distance.

"Is he still there?" she whispered. Joshua hadn't moved. How long had the shooter been there anyway? Hours? Minutes? Seconds? Time had no meaning anymore.

"I don't know." He shifted and she looked up to see him peering out the shattered door. "The shooting's stopped," he said. "Cops are in the garage where the bullets came from."

Her pulse still in overdrive, she straightened and checked Duncan, who'd slept though the chaos. The lobby now swarmed with law enforcement. Kaylee's hands shook and she had to set the baby carrier on the floor.

It finally registered that Joshua was speaking with a police officer. The officer glanced her way then back at Joshua. Finally, the two finished and Joshua returned to her. "I think we can leave. I gave him Clay's contact information, as well as mine and yours. If he needs anything else from us, he knows where to find us."

"Good. I'm ready to go home."

"Then let's go." He picked up the baby carrier in one hand and grasped her elbow with his other. It felt weird and oh-so-right all at the same time. Her husband had only showed her this kind of courtesy when he'd wanted something from her—or he'd wanted to impress people. For Joshua, it just seemed to come natural. She liked that and took comfort from it.

His SUV was still parked in the circle and in short order, she and the baby were safely strapped inside.

When Joshua settled into the driver's seat beside her, she held out her hands, noting the fine tremor still running through them. "Do you think I'll ever stop shaking?" She knew it was shock and that it would pass. The day of her attempted kidnapping, while she'd definitely been scared, she'd also been in so much pain, it had pretty much overridden her fear. Not so today.

He took her left hand and closed both of his larger hands around hers. Warmth enveloped her. "You'll be all right, Kaylee." He glanced into the back seat. "And so will Duncan."

Kaylee desperately wanted to believe him. She nodded and took a deep breath. "I pray you're right."

"Yeah. Me, too."

Joshua pulled away and she clasped her hands together in her lap, missing his gentle hold. "Thank you," she whispered.

"Anytime."

The hour-long drive passed mostly in silence, but Kaylee didn't find it uncomfortable or awkward. The truth was, she was glad he was with her while she processed the terrifying experience. She found herself praying as he drove. She prayed even while she wondered if God was listening. She was leaning toward yes. He'd made sure she'd had help and that Duncan had arrived safely. The bullets at the hospital had only damaged the building. No one had gotten shot or hurt. Yes, bad stuff was happening, but maybe God was still in the midst of it.

When Joshua pulled into the drive of her father's home, the home she'd grown up in, Kaylee tried to see it through his eyes. Traditional in style, with clean lines and a stately bearing, the house really was beautiful. A banner hung between the two white columns that gave it the Southern charm most people swooned over: Welcome Home Kaylee and Duncan!

"Nice," he said.

"Yes. It is. Solid, too. It's been here since the mid-eighteen hundreds. Fortunately, Dad had it restored with all of the modern conveniences of today."

"I was talking about the banner."

"I know." There was no way her father was responsible for that, but she had a feeling she knew who was.

Kaylee opened the door and climbed out. Joshua had put the baby seat behind the driver's side, so he beat her to it.

"I'll carry it," he said when she held out her hand. "From now on, you don't need to be lifting anything very heavy for the next couple of weeks."

"He's only eight pounds," she said.

"Plus the carrier. Lead the way."

The set of his jaw said not to argue. And she didn't have the energy to fight about it. She needed to be wise in the battles she picked. "Okay. Thank you." With a glance over her shoulder, she moved up the steps to the front door. Before she could reach for the handle, the door swung open.

And she came face-to-face with Joshua's mother. "Welcome home!"

Kaylee stiffened but put a smile on her face. The woman looked so pleased and had been nothing but kind to her. Until she proved herself a gold digger, Kaylee would be polite and respectful. Even if it killed her. "Hi." She cleared her throat. "Ah, thank you for the banner. That was very thoughtful."

"You're so welcome. Your father and I were talking about how we needed to do something to celebrate."

Her father? Most likely Olivia had told her father what they were going to do. But he hadn't said no. Interesting.

Joshua simply looked bemused.

Olivia clasped her hands to her chest. "And that awful shooting at the hospital! Coverage is still playing on the television. I tried to call and you didn't answer, Joshua."

"I'm sorry, Mom. I was a little distracted."

"What do you mean? Please tell me you weren't there when it happened."

Kaylee let her gaze meet Joshua's.

"We were there. That's why we're so late getting here. We had to give a statement and answer questions."

His mother's face paled. "How terrible. I'm so glad you're okay."

"We're fine."

They walked into the house and Kaylee once again felt a pang at the loss of her mother. Not only was the woman gone, but everything in the house that had been hers had been put away. Resentment flowed and she drew in a deep breath. "I think I'll lie down for a little while," she said.

"Of course, honey," Olivia said. "Would you like for me to watch the baby while you rest?"

"No." Kaylee's swift answer brought forth a flinch from the other woman. Guilt hit her. "Thank you, though," she said, softening her tone. "I need to feed him."

"Oh, yes, you do that." She smiled but the hurt in her eyes lingered and Kaylee mentally kicked herself. She would not be rude to this woman, no matter her own thoughts on Olivia's reasons for marrying her father.

"It's kind of you to offer. I'm sure I'll take you up on that in the near future. Especially when he's keeping me awake at night."

The hurt faded and Olivia's lips curved into a genuine smile. "Wonderful."

"Where's my father?" she asked.

"He went into the office, but asked me to be here so you didn't come home to an empty house."

"I see." Had he really? Was it possible for him to be that thoughtful? Or had Olivia Crawford just given him the credit to elevate him in Kaylee's eyes? She thought about asking, but couldn't figure out how to do so without it sounding rude.

The doorbell rang and Kaylee jumped. Heart thudding, she swallowed and told herself there was no reason to be so twitchy inside her father's home. She and Duncan were safe here.

Joshua set the baby carrier on the floor as Olivia strode to the door and flung it open.

"Clay?"

"Yes, ma'am. Hi, Aunt Liv."

"Hi, honey. Come on in."

Clay stepped inside and swept his hat from his head.

Kaylee frowned when his eyes locked on hers. The scowl on his face didn't bode well. "What is it?" she asked.

Clay's eyes locked on Joshua's. "You haven't told her?"

Joshua grimaced and shook his head.

Kaylee frowned. "What haven't you told me?"

"I didn't want to spoil your homecoming," Joshua said. "I figured it could wait a few hours."

She was going to strangle him. "What news?"

"Patrick Talbot was released from custody."

A gasp slipped from her lips. "And you didn't think I needed to know that?"

He rubbed a hand across his eyes in a weary gesture. "Of course you needed to know. You just didn't need to know it in the last couple of hours. An officer tailed us here, and I've been on guard, watching. I've seen no sign of him."

Shoving aside her irritation with his silence on her would-be kidnapper's escape, she looked at Clay. "How? When?"

"He was released a week ago. Something to do with a technicality in his arrest and processing."

"But…just…how?" She'd asked that already, hadn't she? And he'd answered her, but her mind refused to fully process the news. Weakness invaded her and she stumbled to the living room sofa. The cushions pulled her in and she wanted to keep sinking until she simply disappeared. But no, she couldn't do that. Duncan needed her.

"Wait a minute. He confessed. And they can just let him go?"

"He recanted his confession, said it was all just a misunderstanding and that he wasn't trying to force Kaylee to go with him. He said she agreed, then at the last minute started going crazy and screaming. He claimed he was about to leave when the cops showed up."

"He was not," Kaylee muttered.

"His lawyer—once he arrived—advised him to just keep his mouth shut. Talbot did. Over the last three weeks, the man's been looking for anything to get his client off. And he found it," Clay said. "It's on video that the arresting officers kept questioning him after Talbot requested a lawyer. It's as simple as that."

As simple as that.

"So, where is he now?" she asked.

"We don't know. No one's been able to track him down. But we're looking, for sure. It's only a matter of time."

"So, what's being done to find him?" Joshua asked.

"Well, he probably had a visitor or two at the jail. I'm going to ride over there today and take look at who's been in to see him."

Kaylee cleared her throat. "So, you think that was him at the hospital today? You think he's the one who was shooting at us?"

"Shooting at you?" Olivia asked. Her eyes widened. "The hospital shooting? They were shooting at *you*?"

Kaylee gave her a short nod and waited for Clay's answer.

"We're not sure," he said. "We've pulled the security footage from the cameras in the garage, but haven't been able to get a good look at the shooter's face. The angles just aren't working to give us that clear shot, however they're still working on it."

"What about the black roses?" she asked.

"Those we know were from Talbot. We got him on camera entering the hospital with the box in his arms. He's also on camera entering your room with them."

She shuddered. "So," Kaylee breathed, "what do I do now?"

Clay placed his hat back on his dark head. "You watch your back and don't go anywhere alone."

Joshua stepped forward and placed a hand on her shoulder. "I'll make sure of that."

Olivia raised a brow, but Kaylee didn't care at the moment.

"Has he used credit cards or left any kind of indication as to where he might be headed?" Joshua asked.

"No. Nothing. Whoever is helping him knows how to keep him under the radar. He's using cash wherever he is."

Kaylee gave a short, humorless laugh. "Wherever he is? I know exactly where he is. He's in Wrangler's Corner, and y'all know it."

Clay rubbed the back of his neck and looked at Joshua. "Yep, I believe you're right about that."

Duncan let out a cry and Kaylee hurried to unbuckle him from his seat. She held the baby in the crook of her arm and turned to Clay. "I don't know why Patrick Talbot is so taken with me or why he thinks black roses would endear him to me." She scowled. "Sometimes being different isn't all that great of an idea. But I'm so sorry for all the trouble he's caused and probably plans to cause it in the future."

"The reasons behind his actions might help catch

him," Clay said. "Then again, maybe not. It really doesn't matter. All that matters is that we catch him."

"Yeah," Joshua said. "And soon."

When Kaylee headed for her bedroom to nurse the baby, Joshua went out to catch Clay before he climbed into his cruiser. "Hey, Clay, wait up."

Clay turned. "Yeah?"

"You think she's okay here?"

His cousin shrugged. "I don't know. Her dad's not here very much. I know he's a workaholic. What about Aunt Liv? How often is she here?"

"A lot when she's not at the boutique. Remember, I haven't exactly been in town to keep an eye on things." More's the pity. "But from our biweekly phone conversations, I've gathered that while she hasn't moved in and she never stays the night, she's here pretty much on a daily basis, cooking meals and cleaning."

"Thought he had a cleaning service."

"He does." Joshua raked a hand through his hair. "I mean, I know they've been friends forever. I know they've helped each other out through some hard times." Like his father's death. "But I didn't realize she was telling herself she was in love with the guy."

Clay quirked a brow. "Huh. Okay."

"Never mind all that. I want to know it's safe to leave Kaylee here. Do you have someone you can put on the house?"

"I can get Trent and Lance and the new deputy to take shifts." Trent Haywood and Lance Green. Joshua didn't know the new deputy.

He nodded. "As long as they understand what's at stake and they'll keep an eye on her."

"They will. I agree that she definitely needs some

kind of police presence here. Maybe the sight of a vehicle in the drive will deter anyone who's thinking she'll be an easy target now that she's home."

Joshua nodded. "All right, that should work."

"But if this guy is determined to get to her, she can't be alone. He's already taken a shot at her. That doesn't leave much room for escalation." Sometimes offenders would start out with smaller crimes and slowly make their way to the bigger ones.

"No," Joshua said, "he's definitely already escalated."

"And he's had a lot of time to think about her, to plan his escape and, depending on his end goal, how he's going to either get even or just plain get *her.*"

"And how to find someone to help him."

"What are your plans while you're here?" Clay asked.

With a raised brow, Joshua let out a low laugh. "Originally, my plans were to come home and talk some sense into my mother about her upcoming wedding."

"You don't approve."

"Are you telling me you do?"

"It's not my business, frankly."

His cousin's unspoken words rang loud and clear. "You think it's not mine, either."

Clay sighed. "Look, man, I know you were devastated when Uncle Don died. We all were. But according to Dad, he encouraged her to find someone else when he passed."

"But it's only been a year!"

"Sixteen months."

Joshua waved a hand and Clay tilted his head, his brow furrowed. "I know it's hard, but like you said, Kaylee's dad and your mom have been friends since they were kids. It's not like they had to go through the whole process of getting to know one another."

Scowling, Joshua sighed. "You're not helping."

"Nope," Clay said. "I'm staying out of it. What I'm not staying out of is helping with Kaylee. I'll get Trent out here for now, and we'll make sure Mr. Martin understands the seriousness of the situation."

"See, that's the thing. His daughter's in danger and he's nowhere to be found. I don't like that quality in a man my mother wants to marry."

"Come on, Josh. Cut him some slack. Have you called to tell him what happened?"

He grimaced. "No."

"And Kaylee probably hasn't, either. You're not being fair and you know it. Maybe he knows he's not welcome and is waiting for an invitation to offer his opinion or express his concern."

That was true enough, but it didn't make Joshua feel any better. "I'm really searching for a reason to object to this whole romance thing, aren't I?"

"Maybe. I'm not saying I don't understand where you're coming from since I'm fully aware of the man's history, but even I can see he's not the same person he was a year an a half ago."

"He's changed that much?"

"Yes. I think he has."

Josh sighed and rubbed his forehead. "I'll think about it."

"Do more than that. Spend time with him. Talk to him. Be the one that helps Kaylee and her father rebuild their relationship."

Crossing his arms, Joshua frowned. "When did you get so smart?"

His cousin laughed. "I don't know. It's just easier to give advice when I'm on the outside looking in."

"Yeah." Joshua jammed his hands into the front pocket of his jeans. "Keep me updated on where this Talbot joker is and if you hear anything more."

"You know I will."

"Thanks."

"Where are you going to be?" Clay asked.

"Wherever Kaylee and Duncan are."

Clay's eyes glinted with something Joshua refused to acknowledge. He'd delivered Duncan and was going to make sure the infant stayed safe. And that meant making sure he had a mother who was there to take care of him.

And that was all.

Maybe if he told himself that often enough, he'd believe it.

FIVE

Kaylee laid the baby in the bassinet she'd found at the local thrift shop. She'd thrown away the old, dirty material that had covered it and found a beautiful print of yellow-and-green pastel. The tiny elephants running across the trim had sold her on it and she'd created the new covering within a few hours.

With a full tummy and a warm bed, all was right in Duncan's little world, and it was up to her to keep it that way.

Someone had tried to kill her. Bullets had come within inches of her and Duncan. And Joshua.

What would she have done without him?

He'd been in the right place at the right time at least twice now. Could it be coincidence? Or could it be God hadn't completely abandoned her as she'd sometimes wondered over the past year and a half?

She sighed and walked to the mirror, studying her reflection as she pulled her blond hair into a ponytail. The last eighteen months had been hard on her, and she could see the fine lines branching out from the corners of her eyes. She probably had a few gray hairs, too, but the blond did a good job hiding them. No, she knew

God hadn't abandoned her. She just wished He'd let her in on the reason her life had taken such a wrong turn.

Because you were stubborn and determined and refused to listen to anyone or anything but your own desires.

First, a father who'd shut her out and turned to alcohol after her mother left, then a cheating husband and, finally, a stalker with murder on his mind? She shuddered and tears welled. What was it about her that attracted the worst of the male species?

Joshua's handsome features flashed before her. His blue eyes that had the ability to freeze the nearest body of water, but could turn warm and inviting within a fraction of a second. Especially when he looked at her son. The fact that he tried to hide it made him even more endearing. Although, she did wonder why he seemed bound and determined to hold her and the baby at arm's length when it was obvious that he cared.

Kaylee lifted her chin and swiped the tears that had escaped. "It doesn't matter why, remember? You are not interested in another relationship right now. For now, you need to survive. And find out if Olivia Crawford is truly in love with your father—or one of the best actresses you've ever met. And while you're doing that, there is to be no romance. There *cannot* be any attraction. Period. Got it?" She continued to look herself in the eye, then whispered, "Got it."

I think. Maybe.

She'd better.

A knock on the bedroom door pulled her away from her mental lecture. She crossed the room and opened it to find Joshua standing there. "Oh! I thought you'd left."

His eyes crinkled at the corners and glinted with concern. She found herself wanting to smooth the lines out and tell him not to worry. *No attraction, remember?*

"Are you all right?" he asked.

Kaylee sniffed and nodded. "Sure. I'm just having a small pity party."

"I see. Is it a private gig or can anyone join?"

A small laugh slipped out. "I don't think you'd have much fun at this party." She stepped out of the bedroom, leaving the door cracked, and headed for the den. Joshua fell into step behind her and they walked in silence to the next room.

Kaylee took a seat on the L-shaped sofa and curled her legs beneath her. The baby monitor sat on the end table next to her. Joshua's mother must have put it there. Not only did it have sound, but a small camera in the room cast Duncan's picture in full color. Her throat grew tight at the woman's thoughtfulness and care.

Or was there an ulterior motive? She couldn't help her suspicions. Brenda had trained her too well.

"There was a woman who started coming around about a year after my mother left," Kaylee said softly. "Brenda Fleming. She came over just about every day, bringing casseroles and little gifts. She was very kind and I was vulnerable. I hungered for a woman's touch, her soft voice, someone to do my hair. Brenda came very close to filling that void for about six months."

"How old were you when your mom left?"

"I'd just turned ten the week before."

"I'm sorry."

Kaylee blinked, fighting the urge to cry. "Things had been tense between my parents for a few months. I'd hear them whisper-arguing late into the night. They never yelled, but I knew something was terribly wrong. However, when she left, I was completely stunned. The stress of whatever was wrong between them was obviously killing her. She'd lost weight, her eyes were sunken into her face and it seemed like she was disappearing right before my eyes." Kaylee wiped an errant tear. "She hugged me, told me she loved me but that she had to leave. I begged her to take me with her, but she said that I had to stay back and take care of my father."

He reached over to hold her hand. "I'm sorry, Kaylee, that's incredibly rough on a kid."

"Hmm. Yes. She died a short time later. My father brought her home and buried her."

"At least he did that."

"At least. Anyway, for a while my father simply ceased to exist. My aunt Carol stayed for a while after Mom died, mostly to take care of me, but she couldn't stay forever. When she left, my dad was around a little more. And he seemed to be captivated by this woman, Brenda, if not necessarily in love with her.

"I was okay with their relationship because I missed my mother dreadfully and my aunt Carol. Brenda stepped in and filled that void to a certain extent. But then one day, she told me that when she and my father were married, they were going to send me to a *lovely* boarding school."

"What?" Joshua's brows dipped.

"Again, my world was rocked. I asked my father about it, and he agreed. Said Benda had convinced him it was for the best. I cried and threw myself at him and begged him not to send me away. Later, I heard them arguing about it—that he was unsure about it. Brenda yelled that it was either her or me, but one of us was going to have to go." Kaylee shook her head and stared at her laced fingers. "I thought she liked me, but she was just using me to get to my father's money."

"What happened to her? Obviously, he didn't marry her."

"I ran her off, I think."

He raised a brow. "What?"

Heat flushed Kaylee's cheeks. "He didn't send her away that day. She still came around, but even I could tell things weren't the same between them. My father and I didn't necessarily get along, mostly because I blamed him for my mother leaving. But it was obvious that he wasn't sure he wanted to send me away. I started being a brat to Brenda and a perfect child in front of my father. I'm sure she told him what I was doing, but there was never any evidence to back up her claims. I was very, very careful and, looking back, I really did terrorize the woman."

"You?"

"Mmm. She hated the outdoors. Any kind of bugs terrified her. I made sure there were a lot of bugs around. One time, I actually put a snake in her car."

"Kaylee!"

"I know, I know. I was horrible. It was just a nonvenomous black snake, but I don't think she knew it from a pit viper. She was hysterical and hyperventilated until she passed out."

"Whoa."

"Once I realized she hadn't actually died from fright, I felt a little bad over it."

"A little?"

She shrugged. "At the time, I just wanted to do whatever it took to make her leave without causing her too much bodily harm. And then, one day, she was gone. I think my father just got tired of her whining and broke off the engagement. He's never said exactly what compelled him to do it, and I've never asked. I heard she married Royce Landers about a year after that."

"The guy who owns Wrangler's Corner Savings and Trust?"

"That's the one. He's twice her age, but that doesn't surprise me. My father was twelve years older than Brenda when they were dating. I guess she had a thing for older men."

"A thing for their money," he muttered then ran a hand over his cheek. He looked up and met her gaze. "Have you had anyone at all in your life you could count on?"

The upturn of her lips surprised her. "A few friends. At the hospital where I worked, there was a group of us who stuck together. Here in Wrangler's Corner, I had a good friend in high school. Natalie Cross. We've kept in touch and have had lunch a few times since I've been back."

"What does she do?"

"She's a lawyer. She works mostly in Nashville and keeps an apartment there, but comes home occasionally to check on her parents. Her mother has dementia, but her dad is handling it for now."

"She sounds amazing. I'm glad she's your friend."

"I am, too." She drew in a deep breath. "And now, I have a decision to make."

"What's that?"

"Natalie's asked me to move in with her. I'm thinking that if your mother and my father are truly going to get married, then I need to give them their space."

He blinked. "They're not getting married."

She raised a brow at him.

"Where does Natalie live?" he asked.

"See, that's the problem. Her place is set out in a remote area right on the edge of Wrangler's Corner. Her brother and his two children live with her—well, they live at her place. Like I said, Natalie isn't there much. Anyway, her sister-in-law was killed in a car accident last year and Natalie's had to help him with the kids—who are three and five years old—when she's there. I think they've hired a full-time nanny so he can work."

"I heard about that. I'm sorry."

"Anyway, if my stalker is going to keep coming after me, I can't move in with her and pull them into this mess."

Joshua sighed and started to answer when his mother stepped into the room. "I'm sorry to interrupt, but I've got some bad news."

What now? Kaylee straightened and took in the woman's pale face. "What's happened?"

"Naomi Anderson just called. Clint's had a heart attack and is being life-flighted to the hospital in Nashville."

Kaylee shot to her feet. "Dr. Anderson! Oh, no!"

"Yes, I'm sorry." Her attention switched to Joshua. "Naomi said Clint was concerned about the practice and his patients. She's calling to ask if you would fill in until he can get someone else."

"Fill in?" Joshua asked. "As in…?"

She nodded. "As in become Wrangler's Corner only doctor."

Joshua's mouth opened but nothing came out. He finally managed to eke out a high-pitched, "What?" He didn't care that it didn't sound very manly.

"I told her I would check with you. I mean, I know you have the time since you took the leave of absence from your practice."

"Yes, but…"

But what? His mother was right. But he'd taken a leave of absence to talk her out of marrying Garrett

Martin. That had been the extent of his plans while in Wrangler's Corner. "Mom, I..."

"Well? You've known Clint since you were two years old. He's one of the reasons you went into medicine. Are you really saying you won't do this for him?"

He opened his mouth, fully intending to refuse. Instead, "Okay, fine. I'll do it," came out.

His mother's face softened and she crossed the room to place a gentle kiss on his cheek. "Thank you, son. I know he'll rest easier and heal faster with that burden lifted from his shoulders."

"Right. But on one condition. It's not a full-time gig. I'll help in any emergency. I'll put in some office hours. I'll help if the nurses run into an issue that they can't handle and I'll take calls from them about prescriptions." A thought occurred to him. If he was going to be working full-time in spite of his part-time insistence, how would he keep Kaylee and Duncan safe?

"Oh," she said, "and you'll have to take care of Clint and Naomi's two dogs."

"Huh? What? Take care of their animals, too?"

"If you don't mind."

Yes, he minded. "No, of course not."

"I'll do the animals," Kaylee said. "Clint and Naomi have been encouraging me to move in to the small apartment off the office. It's right next door to their place. Since I'm not going to move in with Natalie, but plan to go somewhere, that space will work for now. It's fully furnished except for the things I'll need for Duncan. I even know where the key is."

Olivia gaped at her. "Oh, honey, I didn't know you were thinking of moving out."

Kaylee shot her a small smile. "I never intended moving in with Dad to be a permanent arrangement."

"Well, yes, I know. You did say so, but I just thought…" She waved a hand. "Of course, you'd want your own space."

Kaylee had only stayed at her father's home as long as she had because she hadn't wanted to live alone while pregnant. She'd been concerned that she might need something or someone should anything go wrong—or should she go into labor. She almost laughed. Turned out she'd been alone anyway.

And she'd managed just fine.

Well, with Joshua's help. But she hadn't planned on the stalker thing. How could she have?

But she really needed to have her own place. It was time. And if she could help Clint and Naomi at the same time, then that would be her honor. She loved those two dearly. "There are two nurses, me and a woman named Melissa. Between the three of us—and Janelle, the front desk lady—we keep the practice running smoothly. Doc's been looking for another physician to join him, but no one is willing to come to such a rural area. He hasn't given up hope yet, but until then…" She spread her hands and shrugged.

"So, I'm really it, then?" Joshua asked.

"Yes. But don't worry, we'll help you."

"B-but…" Olivia sputtered. "You're on maternity leave. Won't you at least wait a little while? You just gave birth!"

"Trust me, I know." Kaylee gave rueful smile.

"And you're going to need help with the baby," Joshua's mother insisted.

Help would be nice. Kaylee hesitated, but the apartment would be better in so many ways. "I appreciate it, but I'll be fine."

"I think it's a good idea," Joshua said. "I can keep

better watch over you and Duncan if you're nearby. I've visited Doc Anderson a couple of times over the past year, and he's so proud of the top-notch alarm system he had installed. Doors, windows, everything. While the medical offices and the place that would be your home are separate systems, there's a way to program it so you're alerted if anything unusual is happening at the doctor's office and vice versa."

"How does that work?" Olivia asked.

"It's an app you can download on your phone. If something weird happens, it buzzes you. Doc Anderson showed me. I'm sure he'll be happy to fill you in on how it works. Or I can."

Kaylee bit her lip. "I know about the app. Doc mentioned it, but since I'm never there after closing, I haven't had to use it." She paused. "Sounds like you've thought of everything."

Footsteps on the hardwoods reached her ears.

Joshua tensed and Kaylee rubbed her palms over the linen pants she'd donned at the hospital.

Her father was home.

He stepped into the room and his eyes landed first on Olivia. The immediate softening of his features made Kaylee blink. She'd never seen him look at anyone that way. Or had she been too busy being angry at him to really notice?

He walked over and kissed Olivia's cheek then turned to offer his hand to Joshua. To Joshua's credit, he never hesitated. He shook her father's hand then stepped back.

"What are you doing home?" Olivia asked him. "I thought you couldn't get away."

"Well, I decided I couldn't miss my only grandson's homecoming and managed to slip away." He cleared his throat and Kaylee couldn't seem to stop staring. In the few short weeks since she'd returned home, she'd pretty much gone out of her way to avoid the man. When had he started looking all…happy?

"Is he sleeping?" he asked.

"Yes." Kaylee's gaze darted to the hallway that led to the bedroom where Duncan slept. Should she go get him?

Her father sighed. "Oh, well, I always seem to have great timing." He tossed the mail onto the end table beside the recliner, but held a note out to Kaylee. "This came to my office, addressed to you."

She took the envelope and turned it over. She frowned. "There's no stamp or return address."

"Do you have any gloves?" Joshua asked. "Like a pair of latex?"

Her father blinked. "Yes, of course, but why?"

Kaylee watched him, a chill racing over her. "You think it's from him," she said.

"Maybe," Joshua said. "But I want to protect whatever's inside. If it's nothing then you don't have to worry about it. If it's from him, there may be prints."

"What's going on?" her father asked.

"Looks like Kaylee's stalker's back," Joshua said.

The man reared back. "What? I thought he was in jail."

Kaylee rubbed a hand over her face. She really was tired of everything at this point and simply wanted to sleep for a week. "He was released on a technicality. And he shot at us this morning at the hospital."

"Shot at you!" Her father paled and swallowed hard. "Shot at you?"

He was actually worried. For a moment, she simply reveled in the realization. "He missed. Obviously."

Olivia had slipped out of the room and now returned

with a pair of latex gloves that she held out to Joshua. He pulled them on and slid a finger under the flap of the envelope.

He removed a single sheet of paper and unfolded it. "'Living with Daddy won't keep me from you. Soon, my love, we'll be together—for all eternity.'"

Joshua pulled his phone from his pocket. "I'll call Clay."

SIX

Joshua fed Duncan a bottle while Clay talked with Kaylee. He'd arrived within minutes of Joshua's call, having been on his way downtown to investigate a disorderly conduct claim. Sending another deputy to the complaint, Clay now stood in the den holding the envelope with the letter. "I'll get this sent off to Nashville. Hopefully, we'll get an answer in a couple of days as to any prints or whatnot." He turned back to Kaylee. "I've got a deputy watching the house, but this guy worries me."

"What do you recommend?" Joshua asked. He tried not make eye contact with the infant. He was so stinking cute, every time Joshua looked at him, he lost another piece of his heart. He had to keep his distance, keep the baby and Kaylee at arm's length. He sighed. He'd been preaching that to himself for the past few days and yet every time he turned around, he was holding his arms out for the child.

"I think you need to be around someone at all times," Clay was saying to Kaylee. "Or someone needs to stay with you. You definitely shouldn't be alone."

Kaylee frowned. "But that's impossible. People have to work. *I* have to work."

"You're on maternity leave for the next six weeks," Joshua pointed out.

"Well...that's true. Technically. I had planned to help out at least a few hours a day at the clinic. At least... I was." She drew in a deep breath. "But, living in the apartment next to the clinic will make things easier in that regard." She nodded. "I really think that's still the best option in every way. I'll be in my own place and there are people all around all the time. It's within shouting distance of the police station."

"And don't forget the alarm system," Joshua said. He set the bottle down and lifted the baby to his shoulder to pat his small back.

"Exactly. And I'll have his animals. The dogs will bark if anyone approaches the apartment or knocks on the door. I've heard them before."

Clay ran a hand over his hair. "I like the idea of the alarm system and the dogs."

"Kaylee, I don't want you to feel like you have to leave," her father said.

She started and blinked, as though she'd forgotten he and Olivia were there. "I don't really feel like I *have* to. But—" her gaze darted between her father and Joshua's mother "—really, it might be best if I do." Her eyes finally settled on her father. "You're at the office at all hours of the day. Olivia has her own schedule she needs to keep with running her boutique, and this house isn't exactly a hub of activity."

"That's it, then," Joshua said. "You'll move into the apartment next to the doctor's office and I'll be there during the day. At night...Clay, can you assign someone to watch her home?"

Clay pursed his lips then nodded. "I can work the schedule to make sure she's covered at night."

"Don't take this wrong way, Joshua, because I'm not trying to be rude, but I'm not your responsibility," Kaylee said. "And neither is Duncan."

No, the man who should have been responsible had thrown them away like they were garbage. The thought shafted pain through him, and he ignored it. Kaylee seemed to be over the man she'd married, his betrayal killing her love as effectively as anything could have. He studied her and shook his head. He couldn't imagine having her love and tossing it aside as though it meant nothing. He'd only known her a few days and even he could see she was special.

Even if she wasn't for him.

Joshua frowned at the thought and heard the baby burp. He shifted him to the crook of his other elbow. The little guy drifted off again. "I don't see looking after you as a responsibility. I see it as helping out a friend."

She opened her mouth then shut it. Then opened it. "I get that I may need someone to watch out for me. I'm not so naive or in denial that I'll refuse help, but I also don't want to let this guy have control over my life." Her eyes narrowed. "I've been there once. I won't go back to that."

"That's where I come in," Joshua said.

"And me," Clay said. "Well, at least the Wrangler's Corner deputies. Let us do our job. And let Joshua be another pair of eyes. He's got some mad martial arts skills should he need to defend you." He cleared his throat. "Not that it'll come to that. I'm hoping we'll catch this guy before much longer."

Kaylee rubbed her forehead then looked long and hard at Joshua standing there with Duncan in his arms. Joshua couldn't decipher every thought going through her mind, but her rigid stance softened, as did her face. She gave a slight nod. "All right, I hear what you're saying and don't want to be stupid. I would appreciate your help and your watching out for us. I just don't want to live in fear."

"I understand that." Clay stood. "Now, let's see if I can round up a few workers from my church to help get you moved. I just need a date and time."

After several minutes of discussion, they settled on a day next week. He had to admit Kaylee seemed more interested in the interaction between their respective parents than in planning her move. And he had to admit, now that he saw them together, he couldn't help wonder if Clay was right in saying his mother's love life wasn't his business. Maybe the two of them were right together after all.

Maybe.

Kaylee studied her father out of the corner of her eye as she lifted the fork to her mouth. Olivia's pot roast was amazing. After swallowing the succulent bite, she cleared her throat. "Thank you for letting Duncan and me stay here. I know it was a hassle."

Tonight it was just her and her father sitting at the big kitchen table. Two of Wrangler's Corner's finest sat outside. One covering the front and one the back.

"No, it wasn't," he said. "I'm glad to have you here. You're welcome to stay as long as you want." His gruff words reached her and she stared at him. He never lifted his eyes from his plate.

"Oh. Well, thanks."

"But I can see that you may be safer in the apartment near the doctor's office. You won't be alone there as much as you would be stuck out here."

"Yes. I think it's probably best."

He nodded and they fell silent.

"Why did Mom leave?" The question shot from her before she could clamp her lips around it.

Her father stilled. His shoulders straightened.

"I've never asked and you've never said, but I heard you arguing several nights in a row and I just…wondered. Will you tell me?"

He sighed, closed his eyes and raked a hand down his face. "She said it was because she was tired of me being married to my job. That maybe if she wasn't here, I'd come to appreciate her."

"Did you?"

"Yes. And I went after her. But…I was too late."

"Too late?"

He dropped his fork to his plate. The *thunk* rang in the silence. "I don't really want to talk about this," he finally said.

"Well, I do!"

His head snapped up and Kaylee bit her lip. "Too late for what?"

He stood. "Too late to bring her home. Too late to apologize. Too late for everything. There. You happy?"

"No, I'm not happy. I'm not happy at all." She paused. "So, you feel guilty that she died before you got to clear your conscience?"

He swallowed, the blaze of anger snuffed out. "Yes. And no." He tossed his napkin on the table. "I'm sorry, Kaylee, I just can't talk about your mother."

He left the room, his words echoing behind him. But the one thing that held Kaylee motionless wasn't her father's departure, it was his apology.

That was the first time in her life she'd ever heard her father utter those two words—and sound like he meant them.

* * *

The next morning dawned with clear skies and a chill in the air. Fall was definitely Joshua's favorite time of year, but today he barely noticed it. It had been late before he'd finally felt comfortable leaving Kaylee. Only Clay's assurance that he had someone watching the house had given him the impetus to go to his mother's home and get a good night's sleep.

He'd checked in with Clay this morning and felt reassured that nothing had happened during the night at the Martin home. He'd also rounded up some helpers for Kaylee's move.

Progress. He hoped.

With Kaylee taken care of, Joshua was now on a different errand. Five minutes ago, he'd arrived at the hospital in Nashville, hoping to see how Doc Anderson was doing. He stopped at the nurses' station on the cardiology floor. Just as he opened his mouth to inquire as to the doc's location, he spotted Naomi Anderson stepping out of a room three doors down.

Joshua hurried to catch up to her. "Hey, Mrs. Doc." He reverted to his childhood name for the sweet lady. "How's he doing?"

"Oh, Joshua!" Her eyes lit with delight as she stepped forward to buss his cheek. "You're here awfully early."

"Yes, ma'am. I wanted to get here to see if Doc could chat for a few minutes. The nurse I talked to said he was awake."

"Oh, he's awake, all right." She pursed her lips. "And complaining that he doesn't need to be here."

"Worst-patient-ever syndrome?" he asked.

She rolled her eyes. "In spades."

"Maybe I can be a good distraction?"

"I'm willing to give it a try if you are."

He smiled and pushed open the door to step into the room. He found Doc Anderson sitting up in the bed, reading the latest medical journal. "You should be resting, Doc."

The sixty-seven-year-old man laid the journal aside and looked at Joshua over the top of his glasses. "This was just a warning attack, not a full-blown thing."

"Which means you should be resting and taking care of yourself."

Doc grimaced. "I don't have time for this. I have patients who need me."

He meant it. Doc Anderson had taken his medical duties seriously for as long as Joshua could remember.

"I know, sir, and that's why I'm here. If I'm going to take over the practice for a bit, I need you to give me a run-down on everyone."

Doc sighed and ran a hand over his face. "Naomi's put you up to this, hasn't she?"

"I don't know if I'd call it putting me up to it, but yes, she asked."

"That woman…"

"Loves you."

The older man's eyes softened. "Yes, I guess she does."

Joshua's heart did a funny little twist at the expression and he wondered if he'd ever find a love like these two shared. Like his parents had shared.

"I suppose I'm stuck here for a while, aren't I?" Doc said, taking Joshua's mind from the woeful status of his love life.

"For a little while," Joshua said. "You know the drill."

"I know." He frowned. "Doctors aren't supposed to be patients."

"Well, we don't make very good ones, that's for sure."
The man laughed. "All right, pull up a chair."

Joshua did.

"Now, I'm going to start with your most frequent
visitor. Walter Morgan. He's in his early sixties and
sleeps under the bridge. I keep trying to get him into a
psychiatric center, but he won't go. He's a nice fella, but
has some issues. He forgets things sometimes—and not
the things he wishes he could wipe from his memory,
if you know what I mean."

"I do."

"He's got a diagnosis of bipolar disorder. From my
observations, he's not dangerous—to himself or anyone
else. When he's on his meds, he does okay. Actually,
it's like he's a different person. He can hold down a job
and has a wicked sense of humor. I really like him and
wish I could do more for him."

"Not your fault if he won't let you."

"Oh, I know, but I gotta keep trying. Now, on to
young Lilly Adams. She's got type 1 diabetes as does
Zoe Starke's daughter."

"Sophia," Joshua said. "My cousin, Aaron's, daughter."

"You're up on the latest news?"

"Some of it. Especially when it comes to family."

"Of course. Ready for me to keep going?"

"Yes, sir."

While the doctor filled him in on his patients, Joshua
did his best to listen and take notes, but he found his
mind wandering to Kaylee and little Duncan. He
couldn't help wondering if they were safe. Or if her
stalker was watching and waiting while Joshua was at
the hospital.

"… Mrs. Tate comes in."

He blinked. "Sorry, I missed that last part."

"Son, what's on your mind?"

"A lot, Doc." He hesitated. "Is Kaylee a good nurse?"

"Is that what's got you worried?" He waved a hand in dismissal. "Kaylee's a sweet girl and one of the best nurses I've ever worked with. I worked in this very hospital, you know, and I worked with a lot of nurses."

"I know."

"Worked here for a good long time while living in Wrangler's Corner and helping folks on my days off. I wasn't always a small-town doctor."

"I know that, too."

"So, believe me when I say Kaylee's a top-notch nurse. You don't have anything to worry about with her."

Joshua didn't know why'd he'd asked that question. And while it was good to hear, confirming what he already suspected, he wasn't worried about Kaylee's qualifications. Not completely. "I guess I'm worried about her trying to work with a newborn. She's planning to move into the apartment off the office."

The doctor raised a brow. "She is? Well, good for her. Naomi and I have suggested it. With her father getting married, we didn't think she'd want to live there too much longer and, frankly, she needs someone to look after her. Naomi and I had planned on being that someone—or *someones*—but looks like that plan is going to be postponed for a bit."

"What makes you say that? That she needs someone to look after her?"

"I don't mean she's not capable of taking care of herself, just that she shuts people out. Closes herself off. She needs someone to make sure she doesn't isolate herself too much."

"And you think I need to be the person to look out for her? Doc, I'm not interested in romance right now."

The man chuckled. "Did I say anything about romance?"

Joshua grimaced. No, he hadn't. So, why had Joshua?

Doc Anderson turned serious once more. "Just be a friend to her, Joshua. Just be a friend."

A friend. Hadn't he called himself that when he'd offered to help her out? "All right. I can do that. I can be her friend." But that was all.

So, why did the thought of just being her friend make him frown?

"What about Natalie Cross?" he asked. "I know she and Kaylee are good friends."

"Ah, yes, Natalie. She's a good girl, but mostly she depends on Kaylee to keep her on stable emotional ground. She's someone for Kaylee to hang around with and enjoy a chat over coffee, but I'm not sure she'd be very dependable if the chips were down. Not that she wouldn't try, but with that big-time lawyer job of hers, she's never really around." He rubbed his chin, his hand steady in spite of his attack. "I think Kaylee needs you to be her friend. She needs someone she can count on— no matter the situation. You've more than proven you're capable in that role. And besides, it looks like you're going to be family anyway. You might as well start getting along now."

"That's not going to happen, Doc. My mother isn't marrying Kaylee's father."

Doc waved a hand. "That's neither here nor there. And that's between your parents. For now, you need to focus on Kaylee and making sure she's all right."

"I'll see that she gets settled in the apartment." Should he say anything about Kaylee's stalker?

No, not yet. Doc wouldn't know anything about that, and it was clear that he considered himself Kaylee's protector. Joshua didn't want to upset the man if it wasn't necessary.

So, for now, he would take over Doc's role and watch out for Kaylee and Duncan.

As her friend. Everyone needed friends, right?

But friends only. Nothing more. The fact that Joshua had to keep reminding himself of that worried him. A lot. "Her friend," he said and nodded. "I can do that."

"So, when does she move?"

"One day next week, I think. Probably Saturday."

"Wonderful. Keep me updated." The doctor pulled his glasses off and rubbed his eyes. "I hate to admit it, but I'm tiring. So, let's make this quick."

"Of course. Lay it on me."

"First off, I want you to check in on Misty Randall. She had a baby two weeks ago. A stillborn little boy. She lives over off Peace Bridge Road. I've dropped in on her a couple of times and she's in a pretty deep depression. Her husband is using work to escape his own grief, so she's there by herself all day. It's not healthy." He frowned.

"Of course. I'm happy to check in on her. Who else?"

For the next twenty minutes, Doc went through a list of patients, their medications and some personal backgrounds.

All from memory.

Joshua was stunned. As he said goodbye to the doc and Mrs. Doc, he couldn't help evaluating the differences between Doc Anderson and some of the other doctors he'd worked with when he'd done his residency at the hospital. Granted, the patients that had come through that building had come and gone, the doctors seeing them once or twice, but still...the difference in

Doc Anderson and the atmosphere of the hospital blew him away.

And made him think.

As he pulled out of the hospital parking lot, he noticed the black truck that pulled in behind him. His neck and shoulders tightened. Keeping his gaze divided between his rearview mirror and the road in front of him, he took the exit for the highway and breathed a little easier when the black truck kept going.

Between the attack on Kaylee and the hospital incident, he was a tad jumpy.

Joshua pressed the gas, anxious to get back to Wrangler's Corner and to get a start on going over the files. He had log-ins and passwords and patient names to start with. And it looked like he might be delivering a couple of babies in the next few days, as well. For the next fifty minutes, he found himself considering the time he'd be putting in by working full-time. It would completely derail him from his original purpose in returning to Wrangler's Corner.

Funny, he was now more worried about Kaylee and her being a target than he was about his mother getting married. Although, he was still very concerned about that.

He glanced in the rearview mirror and frowned. The SUV behind him had steadily gotten closer over the last mile and was now riding his bumper.

Joshua slowed, thinking the driver wanted to pass him.

The SUV rammed into him.

With a surprised yell, Joshua grabbed the spinning wheel and managed to keep his own SUV on the road even though he had to swerve into the other lane to do so.

Thankful there were no oncoming cars, he moved

back into his lane only to take another hit on the bumper. His heavy SUV skidded to the left. He jerked it back.

Slamming on brakes, he spun the wheel to the right. The vehicle did a sliding one-eighty and came to a stop facing the opposite direction with two tires off the side of the road, spinning in the red mud.

His attacker also hit the brakes, screeched to a stop, backed up and did an expert three-point turn and sped away.

Heart racing, Joshua tried to get the license plate, but it was covered up. On purpose, no doubt. He gunned the engine and the tires spun again, finally finding traction. Joshua shot back onto the asphalt and gave chase. No other cars had been on the road at the time of the attack, and he felt sure the guy had planned it that way. He'd simply followed Joshua until all was clear.

Joshua passed several cars now, but he didn't see the vehicle that had hit him.

The guy had probably turned off the first chance he'd had.

And Joshua didn't have time to go looking for him.

It was very possible that whoever had tried to run him off the road would head straight back to Wrangler's Corner to continue terrorizing Kaylee.

The thought had him pressing the gas pedal a little harder.

SEVEN

In the flurry of taking care of a newborn and packing, it seemed like someone was with Kaylee every minute of every day. Before she knew it, the week had passed and it was time to move. Thankfully, little Duncan was a good baby and had adjusted to a schedule fairly easy. Knowing that could change at any moment, Kaylee was glad to move while he was somewhat predictable.

Thanks to Clay, and his wife Sabrina, mobilizing their church's youth group, the move occurred over a period of about two hours. It went so fast Kaylee didn't have time to think about stalkers or attempted kidnappings. Then again, it wasn't like she had a bunch of stuff. One of the teens had a pickup truck and they'd simply loaded Duncan's crib, several boxes and her suitcases, and that was about it.

But it seemed like she had an entire moving crew slipping in and out of her new home, helping her arrange the furniture the way she wanted it. Teenagers and their parents. Some people she knew, some she didn't. But Joshua seemed to know them all—or at least most of them. "Thank you," she said to the nearest teen. "I can't tell you enough how much I appreciate this."

"No problem at all, Mrs. Martin."

Kaylee startled at her maiden name. And realized she'd just keep it. No sense in trying to explain that Rosetti was her real last name. A name she no longer wanted attached to her—or Duncan. Making a mental note to get that legally taken care of as soon as possible, she started passing out water bottles to her helpers.

And then they were gone.

With one final straggler.

A young woman who looked to be in her early twenties was leaning over Duncan's bassinet, cooing at him. She looked up with a pained smile when Kaylee approached. Misty Randall. Kaylee remembered her from her visits to the clinic. "Hi."

"Hi. I was just admiring your little one."

"Thank you. How are you doing, hon?"

"I'm grieving and sad and mad, but I'm making it." She sighed. "You know people say God has a purpose in everything. Even stuff like losing a baby. I hope they're right."

Kaylee bit her lip, not exactly sure what to say. "Will you try again?" she asked.

"Yes. Eventually." She met Kaylee's gaze. "The doctors say there's no reason not to. They said Gary's death was a fluke thing and nothing genetic, so…" She shrugged. "You're so blessed, I hope you know that."

The vehemence in her voice took Kaylee aback. "Well, yes, I am. In a lot of ways."

Misty relaxed. "Sorry. That came across a bit crazy, didn't it?"

Kaylee laughed at the sheepish look Misty shot her. "Not crazy. Passionate, maybe. But I understand and I'm so sorry you're having to go through this." Kaylee hugged the grieving mother. "Anytime you want to hold a baby, you come see me, okay?"

Tears gathered and Misty sniffed. "Thank you. That might help." She took a deep breath. "Well, I've got to go. I hope you enjoy the new place. I'm sure I'll see you at the clinic before too long."

"Okay, take care. And I'm serious. Call if you want to hold him."

"I will." Misty shot her a sad smile and slipped out the front door.

Once Misty was gone, Kaylee sent up a prayer of thanksgiving. She *was* blessed. In spite of all the craziness going on.

"How's the move going?"

Kaylee turned. "Dad?"

"I had a meeting I couldn't miss, but wanted to come by and see how things were going."

"You wanted to come by and see...? Um, fine. They're going great, actually."

Duncan let out a wail and, before she could move, her father reached the bassinet and carefully lifted the squirming baby. Kaylee popped his pacifier in and his eyes closed. But her father held him to his chest. Stunned, she simply stared.

"He's a good baby, isn't he?" her father asked.

"Yes. I mean, I think so. He's the only one I have any real experience with, but from what I can tell, he's a keeper." She smiled.

Her father laughed. Truly laughed. The corners of his eyes crinkled and everything.

Kaylee blinked. Wow. "You're different."

He met her gaze, his eyes clear and kind, but with a load of regret. "I am, Kaylee. I really am. I want the chance to prove that to you."

She nodded, desperate to believe it. But that would take time.

Kaylee took in her surroundings and inhaled a deep breath. The fully furnished apartment was surprisingly clean for having been empty for several months. She figured Mrs. Doc had probably been taking care of it until they could find a renter.

"Are you sure you want to do this, honey?"

Kaylee started. Since when had Joshua's mother thought it was okay to call her honey? And why didn't it bother her that she did?

She turned to smile at Olivia, who'd just come from the backyard where she'd let the dogs run. "I'm sure. It's for the best."

The woman had insisted on coming along so she could keep up with the baby while Kaylee orchestrated the move. Kaylee had to admit she was grateful. Olivia had shown her nothing but kindness and love. She'd even taken the whole week off from her boutique to stay at her father's house and help with Duncan. Kaylee was starting to have a hard time remembering why she was so opposed to her father marrying her.

Oh, yes. The money. Maybe she was being too judgmental. Or maybe Olivia was just very good at pretending.

She sighed. It would take time to adjust to the idea of her father being married, but she was working on it.

Olivia reached for the baby with a wink and a smile at her fiancé. Kaylee's throat knotted at the love on the woman's face. If she was acting, she was brilliant.

Kaylee's father blushed and let her have the baby. Kaylee had to look away as she realized she was going to have to rethink everything about her father and Joshua's mother. Could someone really change that much? Could another person have that much influence over another?

She had to seriously consider that they truly loved one another and that she was being selfish in her protests.

And, honestly, she had other things she needed to focus on for the moment. The two deputies, who'd escorted them from her father's house, now stood outside the apartment, reminding her that she needed to be on her guard.

Joshua stepped inside and Olivia walked over to him. "Hold Duncan while I grab a bottle of water."

"Of course." Joshua took Duncan from his mother after a brief hesitation.

Kaylee wondered about that. She'd noticed it several times over the past week when Joshua had come by. It was like he didn't really want to hold the baby, but couldn't seem to stop himself from doing so.

Or didn't want to seem rude by refusing.

"I'll take him." She held out her arms and he moved to give him to her but froze when Duncan yawned and snuggled right down against him.

Joshua's face softened and a slight smile curved the corners of his lips. "That's okay. I'll hold him for a little while."

Kaylee's heart tripped all over itself at the sight. Longing hit her hard enough to paralyze her lungs for a few seconds. How she longed for her son to grow up with a father who loved him. A dad who would be a dad, who would spend time with him, loving him, teaching him all the things good dads taught their sons. About baseball and going through puberty and girls. But most importantly…about God. Because no matter how much she might wonder if God had abandoned her, she couldn't really bring herself to believe it. And she wanted her son raised to believe he'd never be alone—no matter the circumstances of life.

The shaft of desperation for that to be, nearly sent her to her knees even as it jerked her lungs into action. She gasped and turned away to gather herself and her emotions.

"Kaylee? You okay?" Olivia asked.

"Yes." She took a deep breath and cleared her throat. "Sure, I'm fine." She turned back to find Joshua's eyes on her. Tender eyes. He'd already fallen in love with her son. The thought thrilled her and scared her all at the same time.

Joshua placed the baby back in Olivia's arms. "I've got a patient coming in shortly. Mrs. Carter just called and said her eight-year-old son fell out of his tree house and has a big gash on his arm. It's probably going to need stitches. I'll be right next door if you need anything."

"His name is Michael," Kaylee said. "He's a rough-and-tumble kind of kid, but doesn't seem to like doctors or nurses too much. Be nice."

"I'm always nice," Joshua said. His affronted look made her laugh.

"He likes you, though," Olivia said to Kaylee. "His mother said you were his favorite nurse."

"He just likes me because I bribe him."

"Whatever works," Olivia said. She turned to her son. "Do you need Kaylee's help? I can stay here with the baby."

Joshua hesitated and met Kaylee's gaze. "It might not hurt for you to be there if you're his favorite nurse. This definitely isn't going to be a fun visit for him. Do you feel up to it?"

Kaylee was tired. From the feedings at night, to the move, to the constant tension of looking over her shoulder for another attack. But she missed her work. The thought of helping Joshua with little Michael energized her. "Sure, I'd love to help."

"Then you come back here and take a nap," Olivia said. "Okay? I think you need it. I've taken the day off to help, so let me do it."

Kaylee opened her mouth to argue and thought better of it. She'd be smart to take advantage of the offer. Sleep was going to be a rare commodity over the next few months. Her body shouted at her to nod her acceptance. "That would be lovely. Thank you."

Olivia's whole face smiled. "Wonderful."

Kaylee went into the master bathroom to freshen up a little. When she returned, she found Joshua and Clay talking in the living area. She didn't see her father.

"...didn't have any cameras on that back road. We may never know who rammed you," Clay said.

"What? Who rammed who? What are you two talking about?" Kaylee asked.

Joshua hesitated.

"What happened?" she insisted.

"Last week, on my way home from visiting with Doc Anderson, someone tried to run me off the road."

Kaylee knew she paled. She could feel the color actually draining from her face. "And you didn't tell me?"

He shrugged. "There wasn't anything you could do about it. I reported it to Clay and got my truck fixed. I never got a good look at the guy's face, but he did remind me of the person who tried to grab you in the middle of the road last week."

She shuddered. She'd been trying to forget that incident. Thankfully, she hadn't had any nightmares about it. Probably because she hadn't exactly been sleeping for long snatches of time. Maybe the night feedings were a blessing in disguise.

The fact that he'd gone after Joshua worried her. Had he thought she would be with him? Or did he just want Joshua out of the way for some reason?

"You ready?" Joshua asked.

She blinked. "Yes. Sorry." To Olivia, she said, "You'll come get me if you need me?"

"Of course. Duncan and I will just go check on the animals and make sure they have food and water." Her voice wasn't quite as perky as it had been before she'd learned someone had tried to run her son off the road.

"Are you sure? I can run and do that real quick," Kaylee said. "I was going to do it after I helped with Michael, but if you think they need attention now…"

"Not at all, I'll just grab Duncan's carrier and he can sit on the table while I take care of the animals." She said the words almost absently, as though her mind was on something else. Like someone trying to hurt her son. Her brows dipped together over the bridge of her nose and her lips turned down in a frown. "Joshua—"

"It's okay, Mom. I can take care of myself."

He probably could, Kaylee thought. In fact, she'd had a front row seat to just how well he could. But no one was invincible. Maybe moving into the apartment would be a blessing in more ways than one. At least if she was close by, she could watch his back, too.

Because it looked like he needed that almost as badly as she did.

Kaylee held Michael's head to her chest and stroked his hair while murmuring soothing words of comfort. At least she hoped they offered comfort. The fact that he didn't fight the numbing medicine followed by the disinfecting and stitching suggested she was doing something right. The promise of an ice-cream cone probably helped, too.

Michael's mother hadn't been able to handle the sight of the blood and Kaylee had sent her from the room so she wouldn't pass out. The last thing they needed was another patient.

"You're doing great, Michael," she whispered.

"Actually, you *did* great, kiddo," Joshua said. "We're all done."

The boy didn't move.

"Michael?" Kaylee said. She moved to back to find him sitting with his eyes squeezed tight. "Hey, it's all over."

One eye popped open. "Really?"

"Yes. All that's left is the big bandage."

He let out a huge sigh and looked down at his wound. "Whoa! That's...wow!"

"Kinda gross, huh?" Kaylee said.

"No way. That's cool!" He turned his arm back and forth, examining it from every angle. "Do I gotta have a bandage on it?"

"Yes," Joshua said in a stern voice. "And you can't take it off to show your friends. If you don't keep it protected for a while, it could get infected. And you *really* don't want that."

Michael looked like he might argue then shrugged. "Okay, then I need a picture."

Kaylee locked eyes with Joshua and she shook her head. If this was what raising boys was like, she was going to need help. But she pulled out her phone and snapped the requested picture. "I'll text it to your mom."

"Awesome." He rattled off her number and Kaylee sent the photo.

Joshua finished with the bandage and Kaylee held

out a hand. "Come on, let's go reassure your mom that you'll live."

"She's afraid of blood."

"Hmm," Kaylee said. "I don't remember her being afraid of blood. She was able to help deliver that foal a couple of weeks ago, remember?"

"Hey, yeah, that's right. Wonder why she got all weird about this little cut?"

His "little cut" had taken fourteen stitches. "Because she loves you," Kaylee said. "Now, come on."

The door chimed, signaling someone had entered the waiting room. Two more chimes sounded. She raised a brow at Joshua. "Looks like we're about to get busy."

"Janelle's got it covered." Janelle Harvey worked the front desk, answering the phone, scheduling appointments and taking payments.

Kaylee squeezed Michael's shoulder. "Come on, kiddo, let's go reassure your mom." She led him out into the waiting room and watched the reunion.

Michael's mother squeezed her son's head to her chest then looked up and mouthed her thanks. Kaylee smiled. An unexpected wave of exhaustion hit her and she swayed.

Whoa.

A hand came down on her shoulder and she jumped. "It's just me," Joshua said from behind her.

"Oh, you scared me."

"Yes, I can see that," he said with a frown. "Why don't you go get some rest while my mom watches Duncan? I can take it from here."

She turned. "Are you sure?"

His gaze darted to the three new people in the waiting room. Two stood at Janelle's window. One sat in the far corner, flipping through a magazine. He looked back at her. "Um, mostly?"

She laughed. At least he was honest. Her gaze lingered on his handsome features. Honesty. What a refreshing quality to find in a man. Then again, that wasn't the only quality about Joshua Crawford that she found herself drawn to.

Kaylee cleared her throat. "All right, then. I think I will go lie down."

The door chimed yet again as she took her first step toward the back of the office.

"I need a doctor. Where's Doc Anderson?"

Kaylee sucked in a breath and immediately regretted it. She nearly choked on the body odor that stole every ounce of fresh air from the room. Walter Morgan. She should be used to the man's almost daily visits by now. But her two weeks off had allowed her to forget the offensive smell he came with. She made her way back to stand in front of him, blocking his path to the patient rooms. "Hi, Walter. Doc isn't here right now."

His face scrunched and his eyes went wide. "Isn't here? But...but he's always here. What am I gonna do now?"

Kaylee's heart went out to him. "Are you on your meds, Walter?"

"Yes. I really am. I just don't feel so good. Kind of weak and shaky."

"I can see you, Mr. Morgan." Joshua extended his hand to the man and never flinched when Walter stuck his dirt-encrusted fingers in his for a brief shake.

"Um, it's okay." Walter hesitated before backing toward the door. "I can wait. I'll, um, just be... I'll just..."

"It's okay, Walter," Kaylee soothed. "Joshua is a great doctor. Michael even liked him. Would you like me to wash out your clothes while you let Joshua take a look at whatever's bothering you?" Sometimes he'd agree, sometimes he wouldn't. There weren't many homeless in the town of Wrangler's Corner as they tended to migrate to the bigger cities, but Walter stayed close and took whatever handouts he could get.

Which included having his clothes washed by Doc Anderson every so often—or by Kaylee since she'd been here.

He hesitated then nodded.

"Good." She patted his shoulder. "You know the routine. I'll get you some scrubs to change into and you can just set your dirty clothes outside the door of the room. Use one of the bags under the counter like you always do. Dr. Crawford will be in to see you shortly." Kaylee jerked her head at Joshua when Walter wasn't looking.

"Ah, right. Yes," Joshua said. "I'll be right there. Why don't you take room three?"

"Three, three. Room three," Walter mumbled as he shuffled his way down the hall.

Joshua quirked a brow at her. "We're a Laundromat, too?"

"Yep."

He nodded. "All right, then. I'll be in room three."

"If you can talk him into it, there's a shower down the hall in the bathroom. It has disposable razors, mini shampoo bottles and other things. Towels are in the closet. Walter knows where everything is."

"Got it." He turned to go.

"Oh!" she said. He turned back, an amused expression on his face. "And sometimes, if we're not busy, Doc Anderson lets Walter just sleep on the table for a few hours then calls Daisy's Diner to order him a meal."

His eyes softened and he shook his head. "I have some big shoes to fill, don't I?"

She smiled. "You're up to it."

He reached out, his hand hovering near her face as thought to touch her. Her breath caught at the look in his eyes. Tender. Soft…and conflicted. Heart pounding at the surge of awareness, she stilled, waiting. A loud thud echoed behind her and the moment was gone. Joshua flinched, dropped his hand, and cleared his throat. "The clothes from room three?"

"Um, yes. Probably."

Joshua pointed with his thumb. "I'll just be in there."

She nodded, glad for the interruption, yet sad, too. What was going on behind those eyes of his? "I'll just… ah…be downstairs putting the clothes in the wash. Then I'll be taking a nap next door." She scooted backward and picked up the bag. "You're going to call Daisy's, right?"

"Yes, ma'am."

She shot him a brilliant smile. Even though his mother may be a gold digger, it looked like her son had his heart made out of the precious metal.

Once Joshua was in the room with Walter, Kaylee took the bag and crossed the waiting room, noticing that the man who'd been sitting in the corner reading the magazine was gone. She frowned. "Janelle?"

Janelle looked up. "Yes?"

"Where's the guy who was sitting there?"

She shrugged. "I don't know. I guess he changed his mind."

"Huh. Okay. I'll be right back. I'm going to toss these in the wash."

Kaylee headed down the stairs to the laundry area. At the bottom of the steps, she paused and shivered as the cold hit her. She'd been down there a number of times and hadn't given a thought about being in the room alone. Now, as the memories of the attacks closed in, her heart rate pulsed faster. The washing machine was straight ahead, but all of a sudden, there were simply too many hiding places in the large area.

Stacks of boxes that held old records—probably dating back to the eighteen hundreds—to her right. Broken furniture and nonperishable inventory on the shelves to her left. An old armoire, wrought iron fireplace tools and a dining room table that had most likely belonged to the one-time occupants of her apartment sat diagonal to her right. The table lay on its side. Someone could easily hide behind it. She couldn't help it, she had to look.

With slow, measured steps, she walked to the table, heart beating harder with each footfall. Finally, close enough, she peered over the edge.

Only to see another box resting behind it. Not the person she was sure was crouching behind it. She pressed a hand to her pounding chest. Scaring herself was not in the best interests of her heart. She was going to give herself a coronary.

"Stop being a ninny," she muttered. "Then again, I have every right to be a ninny, if you ask me." She realized she just qualified for Ninny of the Year. "If you think someone is in the room, you don't go looking for him, you run. Got it? Yeah," she answered herself. "Got it."

The sound of her voice helped settle her, but she detoured to the fireplace tools and grabbed the poker. Feeling better now that she had something resembling a weapon, she strode to the washing machine.

She couldn't help shooting a glance behind her. When nothing alarmed her, she set the poker to the side and with quick movements, upended the bag and let the clothes slide into the washer. Body odor wafted up. She grimaced as she added the soap pod and started the cycle. Poor Walter. He was such a sweet man. She wished life had treated him better. Then again, he'd had the option to get off the streets and had chosen to stay there for whatever reason. Her heart hurt for him and she sent up a prayer for his safety and healing.

A scuff sounded behind her, freezing her for a split second before she grabbed the poker and spun.

And saw nothing.

Pressing a hand against her pounding heart, she listened.

The distance between where she stood and the base of the stairs that would take her upstairs yawned like the length of a football field.

For another few shaky seconds, she stood still and silent, unable to force her feet to move.

Go!

The mental order loosened her from her frozen stance and she darted for the stairs.

Only to skid to a stop when a figure dressed in black stepped out from behind the armoire. "I told you I'd be back."

EIGHT

Joshua pulled the gloves off and tossed them in the red bin. "You'll be all right, Mr. Morgan. You're simply dehydrated. I can hook you up to an IV to get the fluids in you fast, or you can start drinking fluids."

"I don't like needles."

"Then a sports drink it is. We've got some in the break room. I'm going to get you a couple, and you start working on them, all right?"

"Sure."

Joshua headed for the break room. When he returned with the two bottles, Walter was sitting on the table, resting his head against the wall, eyes closed. "You okay, Mr. Morgan?"

"I will be. And you can call me Walter." The man wouldn't meet his eyes. "You're nice, too."

"Too?"

"Doc Anderson, Melissa and Kaylee are all nice. You are, too. Other people aren't nice. It's okay, though, I get it. I know I usually smell."

"Well, you don't smell now. You're clean."

Walter ran a freshly washed hand over his shoulder-length hair and then the beard. "Could use a trim, though, couldn't I?" He'd dressed in the scrubs Kaylee had directed him to and, for the moment, looked like he should be employed at the clinic.

"A bit of one." He paused, popping the top on the drink. "Here you go."

The man downed half of it before Joshua could blink. "Guess you were pretty thirsty."

"I guess."

An idea had been germinating in the back of Joshua's mind, but he wasn't sure he had the right to say anything. And yet… "Walter, I don't know how long-term it would be, but for now, would you want a job? If Doc Anderson says it's okay? I'd have to clear it with him, of course."

Walter's eyes shifted to his then away again. One shoulder lifted in a shrug. "Would depend on the job. I'm not very good at much."

"I don't think you give yourself enough credit. But the job would entail simple things like cleaning up, making sure the doors were locked up, the trash bins empty. That kind of thing."

"Don't you already have someone to do that?"

"Twice a week, but the rest of the time, the staff is kind of on their own. Mrs. Doc usually handles it the other three days, but she's with the doc right now."

Walter picked at a hangnail while he seemed to be mulling over Joshua's words. "What time would I need to be here?"

"We close at five, so around that time?"

The man didn't answer and Joshua wondered if he was trying to find a way to turn him down. Walter pulled a cell phone out of the front pocket of the scrub pants. "Gimme your number and I'll think about it."

"You have a cell phone?"

Walter rolled his eyes. "My daughter insisted on it. She pays the bill each month, and I answer when she calls to check on me. As long as I answer, she promised not to file a missing persons report." He shook his head. "I told her I didn't need the thing, but she convinced me it was for her peace of mind." He nodded to Joshua. "Anyway, number? I have to put it in here. Otherwise I'll forget it. I forget a lot of things these days."

"Right." When he'd taken the oath to do no harm, he'd also promised to do as much good as possible. His gut said Walter was a good man in spite of some of the choices he'd made along his life's journey.

"Until when?" Walter asked.

"What?"

"The hours of the job. From five until when?"

"Oh. Until you're done. Then you write down how many hours you worked, and I'll make sure you're paid."

"How much?"

Joshua opened his mouth to make an offer, but before he could speak, a scream reached him. Not loud, not piercing, but definitely a scream. Like it was muffled. He frowned. "You hear that?"

"Yeah." Walter frowned at the air vent. "Came from there." He headed for the door.

Joshua followed him into the waiting room where he found Janelle hurrying toward the basement door. "Janelle? Did you hear something that sounded like a scream?"

"I heard. It came from the basement. Kaylee probably saw a rat or something."

Fear flared within him as Joshua pushed past her.

Kaylee hefted the poker. "Get back or I'll scream again."

"Scream all you want. You think anyone's going to hear you down here?"

He could be right. *Please, God, help me.* "You were in the waiting room," she blurted.

He took another step toward her. Kaylee didn't back up. She didn't want him to have the satisfaction of watching her retreat. Yet. If he came closer, she would have no choice. If he managed to grab the poker, he could easily take it away from her.

What was she going to do? She had to find a way to get help, but she couldn't hold him off forever.

Pounding footsteps upstairs distracted the advancing intruder. With a glance toward the ceiling, he let out a low curse.

"What do you want?" Kaylee asked. She hefted the poker and actually took a step toward him. He backed up and relief surged. She could do this. "Why me? Did Patrick hire you?"

"Patrick? Patrick who?"

The door at the top opened. "Kaylee? You all right?"

"No! Joshua!"

The man in front of her scowled and headed for the basement exit. "This isn't over," he said as he threw the dead bolt and raced out.

"Kaylee!"

"Down here! Call Clay! He was here." Pulse racing, she ran to the door. The roar of a motorcycle engine caught her attention. He'd parked in the small alley next to the building. He and the powerful machine shot out onto the street and disappeared faster than she would have thought possible.

Footsteps behind her spun her around and Joshua's hands landed on her shoulders. "What happened? Are you all right?"

Reality crashed along with her adrenaline. A tremor shook her and her knees went weak. Belatedly, she realized she was still holding the poker. Joshua took it from her and leaned it against the wall. "I'm all right. It was the man who tried to kidnap me the day Duncan was born."

Joshua blanched and his grip tightened.

"He didn't hurt me," she hurried to reassure him. But he would have. Another shudder ripped through her. "But I need to sit down."

Janelle grabbed one of the discarded waiting room chairs and shoved it over. Kaylee sat and Joshua crouched in front of her. "What happened?"

"He was down here when I came to put Walter's clothes in the washer. I mean, I didn't know it until he stepped out from behind the armoire, but—" she shivered "—he was in the waiting room. He heard the whole conversation about Walter and me coming down here."

"So, he slipped away when no one was paying attention," Janelle said, "and came to wait on you." She paled. "That's so creepy. Who is he? Do you know?"

"No," Kaylee said. She didn't want to get into the previous attack. Taking a deep breath, she rose and Joshua gripped her hand, steadying her. "I'm all right. I just want to go upstairs."

"I'm just going to lock the door." Janelle walked over and flipped the dead bolt then headed for the stairs. "Take your time, don't rush it. You don't want to fall over."

"Call Clay, will you, please?"

"Already had a patient do it. He should be here. I'll send him down."

"Thanks," Joshua said.

Once Janelle was gone, Kaylee wanted to sink back into the chair. Joshua must have had an inkling of the trembling in her knees because he pulled her to his chest. Even as she told herself to pull away, she buried her face in his warm chest. Comfort, safety…and peace…washed over her.

How long had it been since she'd been able to truly relax and trust that no one was going to come after her? She couldn't remember.

Joshua cleared his throat and she jumped back as though he'd singed her.

"I'm sorry, I didn't mean to be all clingy and…" She waved a hand, words failing her.

He caught the hand and raised it to his lips.

Their warm softness sent prickles of electric shocks up her arm and she stilled as goose bumps pebbled her skin.

"I don't mind you being clingy when you've just been scared half to death," he said. "If it were me, I might be a little clingy myself."

She flushed and let out a shaky laugh. "I'm having trouble picturing that one."

He smiled. "Come on, let's go file this report with Clay."

The terror flooded back with a vengeance and she shuddered. "Yes, I suppose we should do that. And we have patients to see."

He slid an arm around her shoulders and led her up the stairs and into the waiting room.

Janelle was talking to Clay, who had his pen scribbling as fast as he could go in his little black notebook. He looked up when Kaylee entered. "Are you all right?"

"I am. I had a good scare, but, yes, I'm all right."

"Good." He looked behind her at Joshua. "You?"

"Fine."

"I called Melissa. She said she'd come finish the

shift. It'll be a good thing when Doc hires another physician and a couple more nurses."

Kaylee winced. Melissa Littlejohn had gamely picked up the slack with Kaylee's recent absence. With only two nurses in the practice, Melissa had probably been run ragged. Kaylee figured she owed Melissa more hours than she'd ever be able to make up. The good thing was the clinic was closed on the weekends and had normal nine-to-five hours. Unfortunately, that left Doc Anderson on call most of the time, but he never seemed to mind. Just said that was the life of a small-town doctor. And he'd chosen it.

Clay turned his gaze back to Kaylee. "You want to tell me what happened?"

Joshua led them into the back to Doc Anderson's office. Once the were all seated with Joshua in the Doc's chair and Kaylee and Clay in the two chairs opposite, Kaylee, spoke.

"I went down to the basement to wash the clothes and when I heard something behind me, I turned and he stepped out from behind the armoire. I screamed, and Joshua and Janelle came running."

"Did he say anything?"

"Not much. I asked him a few questions, but he refused to answer them."

"You actually talked to him?"

"Yes, but like I said, he refused to say much. I was using the poker as a weapon so he didn't have a chance to come at me or anything. Joshua and Janelle heard my scream and came to my rescue. When he heard their footsteps on the stairs, he took off."

Reliving the incident sent shudders through her and she clasped her arms as though that would ward off the chill.

"We need security footage," Clay said. He met her gaze. "Do you know if there are any cameras?"

"Yes, of course. Doc has a state-of-the-art alarm system and has cameras on all four corners of the building." She paused. "Of course, two of those corners now belong to my apartment, but all the windows are armed as well as the doors."

"That's good, but it didn't help much today."

"No, but we can't put a guard on the door to the clinic and do a background check before letting people in."

"Maybe not," Joshua said, "but most of the people who come in here are going to be locals. If Janelle or you and Melissa don't recognize someone, we'll immediately ask for some ID. And keep a close eye on them."

"We can give it a shot," Clay said. "Now that we don't have to have someone on Kaylee's father's house, I can have a deputy in here on a regular basis."

Kaylee sighed and nodded. "All right. That sounds like a step in the right direction."

"I think so, too. I'll see if Trent Haywood can keep an eye on the place the rest of the day. Because while he's watching this place, he'll be watching your apartment."

Joshua blew out a breath. "All right. I've got patients to see. Melissa is here, Kaylee, so why don't you let Clay take you home. My mom can stay with you while you rest. You look pretty done in."

She huffed a laugh. "Thanks?"

He flushed and she couldn't believe she was actually fighting a smile. Clay stood. "I'll get on the security footage. If I get a usable picture, I'll see if my buddy with the Tennessee Bureau of Investigation can get a hit with the facial recognition software."

"Let me know what you find out," Kaylee said. "Please."

"Absolutely."

Because if she didn't know every single detail, she'd probably go stark, raving mad. And unfortunately, it wouldn't take much at this point to push her over the edge.

NINE

Joshua shut the laptop and stood to stretch the kinks out of his knotted shoulders. Everyone else had left two hours ago. He'd been texting back and forth with his mother for the last thirty minutes while catching up on patient files.

She'd assured him that Kaylee, Duncan and Doc Anderson's animals were fine. Kaylee had slept for a couple of hours, the baby was fed, and she was leaving to go have dinner with Garrett. That last part made him grimace. Although, he had to admit that in the midst of all of the craziness, stopping his mother's impending marriage had somehow become the last thing on his priority list. He vowed to rectify that. Tomorrow. Maybe.

A loud thump in the front lobby stilled him. He went to the door of the office and looked down the hall toward the front door. With cautious steps, he moved toward the noise. Another clang sounded, followed by a low grunt.

"Aw, come on, Walter, you know you're not supposed to be in here," a voice said, stilling Joshua's footsteps.

"Am too." A trash bag snapped in the air.

Walter. Joshua's tension whooshed from him in one long breath. He stepped into the lobby to see a Wrangler's Corner deputy standing over Walter, hands on his hips.

"Hey."

The officer spun, his hand going to his hip.

Joshua lifted his hands. "Sorry, it's just me. Joshua Crawford." He cleared his throat. "*Dr.* Joshua Crawford." He noted that Walter had changed back into the street clothes Joshua had brought upstairs. Figuring the man would be back at some point, he'd set them on the sofa nearest the door. The scrubs Walter had been wearing were folded neatly on one of the waiting room chairs.

The officer lowered his hand and straightened his shoulders. "Oh, right. I'm Deputy Logan Williams. You're Doc Anderson's replacement?"

"Just until he's back. Or until I have to leave again." He nodded to Walter. "He's all right. I'd asked him about cleaning up around here a few days a week and a quick text to Doc Anderson confirmed it was fine. Guess Walter decided to accept."

"Yep." The man didn't look at him, just kept working. He'd already pulled the vacuum cleaner from the closet and had a few cleaning supplies set out on Janelle's desk.

"Great. Thanks." He blew out a sigh. "But, ah, today was the cleaning lady's day. She's already come and gone. Do you mind if we move your start date to next week? I'd like to see you feeling better before we start working you." Which was true enough. The man still looked too pale for Joshua's liking. "Are you drinking enough?"

"I think so. I'm running to the bathroom now, so that's gotta mean something, right?"

"Yes, absolutely. That's a good sign." He paused. "Where are you sleeping tonight?"

Walter shrugged and glanced at the couch in the waiting room.

Joshua sighed. "It's going to be in the low forties tonight, Walter."

The man laughed. "I've slept in colder."

"Maybe so, but you're not a hundred percent health-wise. I can put you up at Sabrina's Bed and Breakfast tonight, okay?"

"You don't have to do that." The man's subdued words hit something in the vicinity of Joshua's heart. But since he didn't give an outright refusal, Joshua figured his protest was a token one and that he was desperately hoping Joshua would insist.

"I know I don't. But I want to. Your breakfast will be included and it'll be a good one." Right now Sabrina Starke, Clay's wife, was doing most of the operation of the B and B. If Joshua remembered hearing correctly, Sabrina and Clay had moved into their own place shortly after they'd married. They'd adopted three kids as soon as they could sign the papers then had another one a couple of years ago. Now, Sabrina had resigned from her social work position to help her grandmother full-time at the B and B.

Logan scratched his chin. "I can't leave here or I'd be happy to take him over there."

"It's half a block. I can walk," Walter said. "And be grateful to do so."

"All right," Joshua confirmed. "I'll call Sabrina and get it set up."

Walter walked toward the door. "I'll be back Monday at five." He paused and turned. "Thank you for your kindness." And then he was gone.

Joshua looked at Logan. "What's his story?"

"Former military. Special Ops. His whole unit was wiped out by an IED. He was the only one to walk away. And not only did he walk away, he didn't have a scratch on him. He's never been able to get over the survivor's guilt."

"Whoa." Joshua felt for the man. "What about his family?"

"He has a daughter who comes and tries to talk him into living with her somewhere in South Carolina, but he won't go for more than a couple of weeks. Always seems to find his way back here."

"Any idea why?"

Logan walked to the door and placed a hand on the knob. "His wife's buried in the old community church's cemetery. He won't leave her. Sometimes when I'm patrolling, I'll see him sitting out there next to her grave. Sometimes he's talking, sometimes he's crying. And sometimes he's just staring into the heavens as though wondering what it would be like to join her."

"That's one of the saddest things I've ever heard."

"I know." He offered a small smile. "I can understand it, though. If anything ever happened to Becca, I don't think I'd be able to leave her, either."

"Becca?"

"My wife. We've been married six months." He grinned. "Best six months of my life."

"Congratulations. That's great."

"Thanks. Now, I'm going to do another perimeter sweep and make sure we don't have any lurkers. I'm just glad this one turned out to be Walter."

"I should have locked the door after Janelle left, but got involved in paperwork and didn't think about it." Actually, he'd just assumed Janelle would have locked it. She'd only been gone about ten minutes before Walter had arrived. However, in the future, he'd be more careful."

Logan nodded and slipped out the door.

Joshua blew out a slow breath and decided to look in on Kaylee before heading home. He double-checked the doors and the alarm before stepping onto the porch. Once he had the door shut behind him, he twisted the knob. Locked. Perfect.

He walked down the steps and walked down the short sidewalk that led to Kaylee's new apartment. The apartment and the medical office were connected, but he preferred to knock on her front door instead of the connecting door inside.

Standing there, hand raised to knock softly in case Duncan was asleep, he felt the hairs on the back of his neck prickle. Looking over his shoulder, he saw Logan Williams climbing back into his cruiser. The deputy saw him watching and raised a hand.

Joshua responded with the same gesture yet couldn't stop his gaze from sweeping the area. Something just didn't feel right and it frustrated him that he couldn't put his finger on it. But he knew one thing: he wasn't leaving Kaylee alone tonight. Before he knocked, he was going to check a few things out himself.

Kaylee took her friend's empty mug and walked to the coffeepot to pour her another cup. When she returned, she set the drink in front of Natalie, who was seated at her kitchen table. "Thanks for stopping by. I'm really glad you had time."

"Of course. I've been dying to see this little one." She held a sleeping Duncan in the crook of her arm. "Work has just kept me so busy, I haven't had a chance to breathe. A new case has landed on my desk and it's an interesting one, but very time-consuming."

"No worries. I understand."

Natalie bit her lip. "So, how are you doing? Really?"

Kaylee sighed. "I'm doing okay," she said softly. One of Doc's dogs, Bonnie, slipped over to rub against Kaylee's arm. She scratched his ears while she pondered how much to tell Natalie about what was going on in her life. Right now, the topic was Kaylee's dead husband.

"I can't believe what Tony did," Natalie said. "Cheating on you, throwing you out, rejecting—well, I can't believe it. And I can't believe he's dead. I can't believe *how* he died." She paused. "Apparently, I can't believe a lot of things."

"Believe it. All of it."

"I'm just so sorry."

She patted her friend's hand. "I know. You've told me a million times."

"But I feel so *responsible*," Natalie wailed. "I introduced you."

"Because I twisted your arm."

They'd been at a hospital fund-raiser, one that the Rosetti family had given quite a bit of money to, and Tony had been there, taking advantage of the generous buffet table. Kaylee had seen him and been instantly drawn to his dark good looks. She'd simply watched him for a while until she'd seen Natalie talking to him like she knew him. Kaylee had made a beeline for her friend and wrangled the introduction.

"I made my own choices when it came to him. You may have introduced us, but, as I recall, it was begrudgingly and you told me not to have anything to do with him because he wasn't trustworthy. I chose not to listen to your sound advice and, as a result, I suffered the consequences. You have nothing to feel responsible for."

Natalie gave a light snort. "That doesn't make me feel much better." She paused. "Okay, maybe it does. A little."

"Well, that's your choice and you're responsible for it, not me."

Natalie grimaced and stuck her tongue out at Kaylee. Kaylee grinned. She couldn't help it. Natalie was tall and brunette, with green eyes that could sparkle with mirth or pin one to the wall when she was arguing a case. Her razor-sharp mind often took people by surprise. People who made the mistake of casting stereotypes.

Her friend sighed. "If he'd died in that car accident, you wouldn't be in this situation."

Kaylee raised a brow. "What do you mean?"

Natalie shrugged. "I mean you'd still be a single mom with a dead husband but… You remember when that drunk driver slammed into him and put him in the hospital?"

"Of course I remember. It was right after Tony got out of prison for the drugs. I had just told him I was pregnant and he'd told me to get out. But what does that have to do with anything?"

"And you still showed up at the hospital."

"I had to. He was still my husband."

Natalie shrugged. "I don't know. At that point you were still getting along with your in-laws."

"Because neither Tony nor I had told them anything."

"I know, but even so."

Kaylee shook her head. "No, Tony's mother started acting weird after that accident. It was like she thought I was to blame for it or something. I'd never seen her so worked up about him. She'd never seemed to care that much." She gave a low, humorless laugh. "She didn't even know her own son's blood type."

"What do you mean she blamed you?"

"She found out Tony was coming to the hospital and thought it was to see me. She actually said I shouldn't have been working. That I should have been at home so Tony wouldn't have felt the need to go out that night."

"What?" Natalie's green eyes shot bits of fire. "That doesn't even make sense!"

"Tell me about it. She knew Tony came to see me at the hospital often." Her jaw tightened. "Of course, we now know it was really his mistress he was coming to see, but nevertheless, he hadn't told his mother this. So, she managed to place the blame on me and leave it there."

"Of course."

"And then there was one other weird thing. When she walked in and found me looking at Tony's chart, she went ballistic."

"Why?"

"No idea. She just slammed the laptop shut and told me to mind my own business."

"You were his wife! He *was* your business! Not only that, but you're a nurse. Who better to know what's in his chart?"

"I know. Like I said, it was really weird. Before the accident, she at least talked to me. But after? She went out of her way to avoid me. Or suggest I not come over to dinners or whatever. I don't know. It was like she really didn't want me around anymore."

"Wow. All because of Tony's accident?"

"Apparently." Kaylee still didn't understand it. "And

then when he died…well…let's just say, I really wasn't their favorite person at all."

Natalie sighed. "I'm sorry. I just wish things were different for you. I wish Tony had been different."

Kaylee sighed. "Yeah. You and me both."

A knock stiffened her spine as the dogs barked and ran to the front door.

Who could that be? Flashes of Patrick Talbot's letter sent a tremor through her. And then the memory of her attacker clutched at her. Surely, neither would just walk up and knock. Right? She moved to the door and peered out the window only to release her breath in a huff of relief. Joshua. She opened the door. "Hey."

"Hi. You mind if I come in for a few minutes?"

"Of course not."

Once inside, he spotted Natalie sitting at the kitchen table. She waved and he flushed. "I'm sorry, I didn't realize you had company."

"It's fine," Kaylee said. "This is my friend, Natalie Cross. Natalie, this is Joshua Crawford. Come join us."

"I remember you from high school," Joshua said, shaking Natalie's hand. He smiled. "Good to see you again."

"Thanks. You, too."

"Would you like some coffee?" Kaylee asked.

"Sure. If it's decaf."

Natalie stood. "I have to get going." She held the baby out to Joshua, and Kaylee noted there was no hesitation this time when he took him. Natalie then turned to hug Kaylee. "I'll try to stop in again sometime next week when I'm back in town."

"That would be lovely, but you don't have to leave unless you just need to," Kaylee said.

Dear Reader,

IT'S A FACT: if you answer 4 quick questions, we'll send you 4 FREE REWARDS!

I'm not kidding you. As a leading publisher of women's fiction, we value your opinions... and your time. That's why we are prepared to **reward** you handsomely for completing our mini-survey. In fact, we have 4 Free Rewards for you, including 2 free books and 2 free gifts.

As you may have guessed, that's why our mini-survey is called **"4 for 4".** Answer 4 questions and get 4 Free Rewards. It's that simple!

Thank you for participating in our survey,

Pam Powers

To get your 4 FREE REWARDS:
Complete the survey below and return the insert today to receive 2 FREE BOOKS and 2 FREE GIFTS guaranteed!

"4 for 4" MINI-SURVEY

1 Is reading one of your favorite hobbies?
☐ YES ☐ NO

2 Do you prefer to read instead of watch TV?
☐ YES ☐ NO

3 Do you read newspapers and magazines?
☐ YES ☐ NO

4 Do you enjoy trying new book series with FREE BOOKS?
☐ YES ☐ NO

YES! I have completed the above Mini-Survey. Please send me my 4 FREE REWARDS (worth over $20 retail). I understand that I am under no obligation to buy anything, as explained on the back of this card.

❏ I prefer the regular-print edition
153/353 IDL GMYM

❏ I prefer the larger-print edition
107/307 IDL GMYM

FIRST NAME	LAST NAME

ADDRESS

APT.#	CITY

STATE/PROV.	ZIP/POSTAL CODE

"Please—" Joshua frowned "—don't let me chase you off."

Natalie gave a small laugh followed by a rueful smile. "Don't worry, you're not. I've got a court case coming up, and I need to look over some new information that landed in my inbox earlier. I stayed longer than I should have already because I didn't want to give up that sweet bundle of love. But now I'm out of here."

"If you're sure," Kaylee said.

"I'm sure. See you soon." Natalie's eyes softened when they landed on the baby in Joshua's arms. "Tony may have been a louse, but you got one good thing out of that marriage."

Kaylee blinked and gave a sad chuckle. "Yes, I can't even regret marrying him too much when I look at Duncan."

"All right. Later." Natalie zipped out the door and Kaylee waved Joshua to the den.

Joshua took a seat on the couch, Duncan's warm weight becoming something he missed when he wasn't around. He tried to harden his heart, but just didn't have the energy tonight. He'd do better tomorrow. Bonnie and the other dog, Rufus, joined them and settled in front of the fireplace. The coziness of the whole scene got to him and his heart started to long for things it shouldn't.

He leaned his head back and closed his eyes to shut out the picture. Only, it didn't go away. He could still see the whole scenario in vivid color. His imagination even added Duncan at about six years old, playing on the rug with a toy car.

Reining in his runaway thoughts, Joshua forced himself to simply enjoy the moment of holding the baby and just...being.

In a moment, the cushion next to him dipped and he figured Kaylee had joined him. All relaxation fled as he realized he was hoping she'd snuggle up next to him.

"Tired?" she asked from a safe distance. He squashed his disappointment.

"A bit." He rolled his head to look at her. Her quiet beauty struck him again. Not just physically, but in every way. He'd misjudged her. She was kind, thought of others first, had compassion for those less fortunate, like Walter Morgan, was brave in the face of real danger...

He realized he was staring. "Today wasn't the reason I came home. It's not what I came here to do and, while I enjoyed it, I need to find my focus."

"So we can stop the wedding?"

"Yes."

"I don't think that's going to happen."

He sighed. She was probably right. "Your dad isn't the monster I pictured him. He isn't the man I remember."

"I know. Your mother isn't the gold digger I was afraid of."

A low laugh escaped him. "Would it help if I told you that my father left her pretty well-off and she doesn't have to marry again if she doesn't want to?"

"So, she has the boutique just for something to do?"

"Yep. After Dad died, she was lost. She'd always helped him do his books. She's a CPA and that's what she did full-time before they met. After they married and had me, she wanted to do more than just stay home after I was in school."

"So your dad let her work for him."

"Yep. Part-time mostly, but he was her only client, so it worked out."

Kaylee leaned her head back against the couch, as well. "You're so fortunate to have had your mother this long. I love my father, but I miss my mom with an ache that sometimes I don't think will ever heal."

"I'm sorry." He reached over and clasped her fingers then dropped them. What was he doing? Sitting on her couch, holding her baby?

Wanting to kiss her?

But he did. Want to kiss her.

And he wanted to keep her safe. The incident in the basement of the clinic was still fresh in his mind. Someone was out to hurt her, and he needed to keep his thoughts on that and not on how her lips would feel against his. Or how right her baby boy felt nestled in the crook of his arm. Or wonder what it would be like to see Duncan on a regular basis.

Because if he didn't focus on something other than those things, he was going to lose his heart before this was all over.

Kaylee tried to read his odd expression and found herself at a loss.

He cleared his throat.

"You know how I said I didn't mind you being clingy when you've just been scared half to death?"

"Yes."

"The truth is, you don't have to be scared to death." She blinked. "Huh?"

"To be clingy. You can be…not scared to death. If you want."

His sweet, fumbling way of telling her she could depend on him brought tears to her eyes. Leaning over, careful not to wake the sleeping baby, she pressed a kiss to those soft lips she'd found herself dreaming about.

He didn't move. He wasn't responding, but he didn't pull away, either.

Feeling foolish, she started to retreat only to have his hand slide to the base of her head, tugging her closer for another sweet kiss.

This one he took control of.

This one sent a flush from her toes to her forehead.

And it was entirely too short.

When he lifted his head, his eyes met hers. "I like you, Kaylee. A lot."

Her heart did that little flippy thing it wanted to do whenever she was in his presence. "Um, good. Thanks. I like you, too. A lot. Obviously." She wanted to groan. Was she even making sense with her choppy wording?

A slight smile curved his lips. "I'm glad." Then he frowned.

"Uh-oh," she said.

"What?"

"The frown."

He raised a brow. "Oh. That wasn't for you."

"What was it for then?"

"I'm just worried that I'm…that we're…that you're…" He huffed a sigh and looked away.

"What?" she asked.

He stood and paced to the mantel. "A distraction," he said softly.

"Oh." The sharp hurt surprised her.

He raked a hand through his hair. "That didn't come out right."

"Then I *shouldn't* be clingy."

A wince. "That's not what I meant. You're a wonderful distraction. You and Duncan both. But I…"

"What?"

"I'm just not sure about a lot of things in my life right now, and I don't want that to spill over onto you. And have it wind up being a negative thing."

"I...see."

"No, you don't."

"Then help me."

He sighed. "I've got my life planned out for the next few years. I've got this MMA competition coming up. If I win, I'll have enough to pay off my school loans and then open my own practice in Nashville."

"That sounds like a wonderful plan." And it did. But she saw where he was heading with his explanation. It didn't sound like he had room for anything or anyone else.

"Thanks." He returned to sit beside her and stroked her cheek. She simply watched him while trying to figure out what she wanted to say.

"I don't trust many people," she finally said. "Not men, not even women, after witnessing how some of my in-laws behaved." She tilted her head. "But I trust you."

"Why?"

"I don't know. And that scares me a bit. As you've probably figured out from my choice in husbands, I have lousy judgment."

"You and me both."

She lifted a brow. "Who hurt you?"

"Ginny Overland. A woman I met on the MMA circuit. She had a little boy named Christopher. He was two and thought I was the greatest thing ever. I thought he was, too. We spent all our spare time together—which wasn't a whole lot because I was going to medical school, too, but we managed. Then one day, Ginny decided Christopher needed to be with his father—with

his real family. She asked me not to come around anymore because Christopher needed to adjust to the new
people in his life and I needed to simply fade out of
the picture."

"Oh, Joshua, I'm so sorry."

"I was a mess. I loved Ginny, and I loved that kid
like he was my own." He looked down at Duncan. "And
now I find myself in a situation with the potential to
be very similar."

"Except Duncan's father is dead."

"I know. But he still has family. Blood relatives."

She snorted.

He flushed. "I'm sorry. I'm just thinking out loud. I
need to zip my lips and go home. I come with baggage,
Kaylee, I guess is what I'm trying to say. So, maybe you
should run away from me. Run far away."

"Is that what you want me to do?"

His expression didn't allow her to see past the color
of his eyes. Then his lids lowered. "No. If I'm honest, I
want to stay right here with you and Duncan and keep
getting to know you while we keep you safe from your
stalker. I guess I'm just being whiny and afraid of being
hurt again. That's all. You can laugh now."

She reached for his hand, squeezed. "I'd never laugh
at you. That would be mean after you've been open and
honest. So let me just put your mind at rest.

"Duncan will never have anything to do with his father's side of the family. Not as long as there's breath in
my body. Except maybe Marla and her husband. Marla
is Tony's sister. They were nothing but kind to me, especially after they found out I was pregnant and Tony
had kicked me out. They were furious with him. But
his parents?" She shook her head. "They blame me for
his death."

Joshua frowned. "What? Why?"

"Because when I found out he was cheating, and who he was cheating with, I told her husband."

"Ouch," Joshua said.

"I mean, I didn't set out to tell him. But he approached me in the grocery store one afternoon and asked if I thought something was going on between his wife and my husband. I said I did and explained that Tony had left me for her, kicking me out of the house in the process."

She shuddered. "He was furious and threatened to kill them both. I called Tony to tell him that I was afraid the woman's husband was dangerous and that he'd made the threat." She swiped a tear. "Tony laughed at me and told me to get over my petty jealousy, that we were done. So, I called the cops and told them. They said they really couldn't do anything with just a threat, but would go to the house and talk to the husband. Later, they told me that he seemed perfectly congenial, understandably upset, but not homicidal, and that he didn't own any weapons."

"And then he killed them."

"Yes—with his brother's gun. Like I said, Tony's parents blame me for all of that."

"That's crazy."

"Maybe. And while their hatred of me is a valid enough reason to keep Duncan away from them, it's not the only reason."

"What's the other reason? I mean it's not like they're criminals, are they?"

This time she did laugh, a short, humorless, hiccuping sound. "Yes, actually, they are. They're worse than just criminals—they're organized crime."

TEN

Joshua wasn't sure how long his jaw hung swinging loose, but he finally snapped it shut. "Kaylee, seriously?"

"Unfortunately." She sighed. "I didn't know it at the time I married Tony. He left that little detail out from all of our long superficial talks."

"I see. That's just…wow."

"I know." She pressed her palms to her eyes. "I was so stupid. This was all less than two years ago, and I feel like I've grown up and matured exponentially since finding out the truth about Tony."

"What drew you to him?"

"He was good-looking, and he made me laugh." She peered at him from beneath her lashes and he could see the self-loathing there. It made his heart hurt in a way that took him by surprise. And yet didn't. Kaylee had managed to wiggle her way under his skin, and he knew he cared about her more than he should.

"He made you laugh."

"Yes." Another sigh. "He was always joking around. I know it's silly, but once Mom died, so did the laughter in my life. Dad turned to work to bury his grief. He couldn't stand for me to be around because I look like Mom. As a result, he completely withdrew from me and relied on the alcohol to dull his loss. I didn't lose one parent, I lost two. And I felt utterly alone and unloved. Tony not only made me laugh, he made me feel loved again. At least for a short time."

Joshua slid his free arm around her shoulders and drew her to him. She rested her head against him and he swallowed at how right she felt there.

"What if it's them?" he asked.

"What do you mean?"

"What if it's not a stalker? What if it's your dead husband's family who's trying to kill you? Because they blame you for his death?"

She let out a laugh, one without much humor. "No, I seriously doubt that. They had basically disowned him even before we'd met. Tony has a brother and a sister who are the golden children. He would often bemoan the fact that he could never seem to do anything right. So, he married me to get back in their good graces."

"How was that supposed to work?"

"They wanted him to marry someone reputable, a girl from a good family, that could be used to…" She waved a hand, searching for the words. "I don't know… to bring a better light to their name or something? Does that make sense?"

"Completely."

"Good. And even though I wasn't the girl they had in mind, at first it seemed to work. They liked me and I got along well with them. I'm sure they liked the fact that my father had money and an upstanding reputation in the business community in spite of his reputation of being a drunk." She shrugged. "As long as he was making people money, they didn't seem to care how much he drank." She waved a hand. "Anyway, all was well for the first few months. And then Tony started staying out all night. He said he was working, but he wasn't very careful about the clues he was leaving behind. A receipt to an expensive restaurant. A hotel bill when there should have been none." She shook her head. "I was innocent and naive about a lot of things, but I wasn't stupid. And then he was arrested for possession."

"Oh, Kaylee. I'm sorry."

"I was, too. However, he was still my husband. I'd promised for better or for worse. I thought being pregnant might wake him up or something. So, I bailed him out of jail and told him I was expecting his child. He was furious. Told me to get an abortion."

Joshua's sharp intake of breath soothed the raw feelings that surfaced at the retelling of one of the worst moments in her life. "I refused and things went downhill from there. One night, I followed him and caught him coming out of a restaurant with another woman on his arm. I gave him a choice—an ultimatum, really—that if he wanted to stay married, he would come home. If he didn't, then to tell me so." She clasped her hands and shook her head. "And, he told me so. More specifically, he told me to get out of his house. So, I did."

"I'm sorry, Kaylee." He shook his head. "I keep saying that, but I am. So very sorry you had to endure that."

She fell silent then sighed. "I'm sorry, too. About a lot of things. Like being so gullible and falling for his fake charm and smooth lies." She touched her still-sleeping son's downy cheek. "I'm sorry he'll never know or understand what he could have had. I'm sorry it ended the way it did. For him and the woman he was involved with. They were very wrong in what they were doing, the way they were living, but they didn't deserve that."

"Yeah. What about Talbot? What was his family like? Do you know?"

She shook her head. "I know that his parents are deceased and he's the youngest of four. He has two sisters and a brother. One of his sisters came to me and begged me to drop the charges. She promised to get Patrick help if I would drop the charges."

"But you didn't?"

"No way."

He squeezed her fingers. "Good job."

She gave him a shaky smile. "Thanks."

Duncan stirred and opened his eyes. Joshua looked into them. The baby blinked—then scrunched up his face and let out a wail that made Joshua jump.

"Wow," he laughed. "Nothing wrong with his lungs."

"He's hungry. Let me just get a bottle and we'll take care of that."

Thirty minutes later, Duncan was full, changed and looking around with curious eyes while he sucked on three fingers of his tiny right hand.

"I guess it's time for me to leave," Joshua said.

He hated to go. The realization hit home for him as did the fact that the more he was around Kaylee and Duncan, the more he wanted that to continue. He'd faced a lot of things in his life that had scared him in more ways than one. But knowing that Kaylee now had the power to break his heart wanted to send him running. He stood and handed her the baby. "Are you going to be all right?"

"Sure."

She'd answered too quickly.

"I know Logan is watching your place part of the night," Joshua said, "and I think Lance comes in the later part until morning."

"I'll be fine." She held the baby tucked against her shoulder, and Joshua followed them to the door.

"All right, then, good night."

"Good night."

His gaze dropped to her lips and he almost leaned over. Instead, he caught himself and told himself not to encourage something that was bound to hurt one or both of them. He offered her a tight smile and slipped out the door.

Kaylee couldn't get Duncan to sleep no matter what she tried. The baby was determined to stay awake. He alternated between being happy and cranky. She'd already paced grooves into Doc Anderson's pretty wood floors, had tried swaddling Duncan and walking with him, and had offered him another bottle. All to no avail. He was full, he was dry—and he was still screaming. Maybe he just needed to cry. Maybe his little tummy hurt. All she could do was pace and rub his back.

And sing. Probably a little off-key, but it seemed to work.

After the first few notes, the baby fell into a hiccuping pattern that slowly faded and he dropped off to sleep. Finally.

Weary, she realized she'd been so focused on Duncan, she hadn't thought about her stalker. With a sacked-out Duncan resting on her shoulder, she walked to the window and peered out. The sight of the Wrangler's Corner cruiser sitting at the curb allowed her to relax enough to slip into the bedroom and place Duncan in his bassinet. He promptly shoved his three fingers into his mouth and she froze, thinking he was going to wake up screaming again.

When he didn't, she let out a low breath and closed

her eyes. Yes, she was tired. Brain-dead tired. Between the move, the attack at the clinic and Duncan's irritable personality tonight, she was completely done in.

Kaylee managed to shower and wash her hair before pulling on sweat pants, a long-sleeved T-shirt and heavy socks. While Duncan slept, she, too, would sleep. She crawled into bed and pulled the covers up. And drifted.

Noise jerked her out of her light doze and she sat up, confused, disoriented, blinking. Kaylee rubbed her eyes and got her bearings. She was in her new home. Duncan was asleep in the bassinet. Everything was fine.

So, what had awakened her?

She walked over to peer into the bassinet. Duncan still slept soundly, his little fingers still in his mouth. Maybe the sucking noise he made had pulled her out of her restless sleep.

Or not.

Quietly, she moved through the small apartment, checking each window and every door. Nothing seemed out of place. Everything was locked. And the alarm was armed. Shaking her head, she turned to go back to her bedroom, deciding her restlessness had to do with a combination of things like a new place, the fact that her stalker was still out there and she—

What was that?

A footstep?

In her home?

No, the alarm was set. And there was someone watching her house. There was no way someone could get in without her and Logan knowing about it. Could they?

Stomach twisting, she bit her lip and hurried back to the bedroom. She'd gather Duncan and her phone and get Logan's attention. She hated to be so needy and afraid, but figured she had good reason to be. Next to the bassinet, she reached for the baby only to stop. And blink.

He wasn't there.

But that was impossible.

A scream gathered at the back of her throat and she held it in by sheer will. She ran to the front door and threw it open. The alarm blared, but she ignored it. Logan came running to her—followed by Joshua?

When he reached her, he gripped her upper arms. "What is it? What's wrong?"

"Duncan's missing. He's gone." Saying the words made it real. Grief and fear crashed through her and, if he hadn't been holding on to her, she would have hit the ground.

Joshua paled. "That's not possible. We've been sitting here for hours. No one's approached." He led her inside and shut the alarm off. They left Logan talking on his radio while Joshua bolted for her bedroom. When he looked into the bassinet, he staggered backward. Looked at her rumpled bed, then back to her. "He's not here."

"I know that!"

He raked a hand through his hair. "But how?"

"That's what I want to know," Logan said from behind them. Kaylee whirled and found him in the doorway, hands on his hips. "A baby doesn't just disappear."

But hers had.

Clay wasn't messing around. Within the hour, he had the FBI involved. Special Agents Henry Gilstrap and Mike James. Two men with hard eyes and unflappable expressions. They immediately took over Kaylee's kitchen as their command center, ready and waiting for any kind of ransom call.

Clay and Deputy Logan Williams had searched every corner of the small apartment as well as the attached doctor's office. The alarm had been armed until Kaylee had set it off by running out the door. Right now, she paced in front of the mantel, her hair pulled back in a messy ponytail. She wore sweats and a T-shirt and slip-on tennis shoes. She was ready to act when the word came about Duncan.

Joshua stood next to Clay. "I'm ready to give her a sedative if I have to."

"Not yet. I need to talk to her."

He approached, and Joshua stayed on his heels. Clay placed a hand on Kaylee's arm and she spun.

"Did you find him?"

"Ah. No. Not yet. I was wondering if you could answer a few more questions."

"Of course."

"Kaylee, you've been through a lot the last year. The last two years, really. Think back over those last two years and try to think of anyone who has it in for you besides Talbot. This just doesn't make sense. He had access to you if he had access to Duncan. He took the baby and left you alone."

She blinked at him. "You don't think it was Patrick who did this?"

"I don't know. His gifts, his letters, they all point to his fixation on you. He's never mentioned the baby. Like I said, this doesn't match up. So, let's just assume for the moment that it's not Talbot. Can you think of someone else who might have it in for you? It doesn't matter how small or insignificant you think something is, I want to know about it. Did you cut someone off in traffic? Make a patient—or parent of a patient—mad about something? Anything?"

Kaylee blinked at him, but didn't answer right away. Joshua took it as a sign that she was thinking. Hard. Finally, she simply shook her head. "I don't know."

"Her in-laws," Joshua said.

"What?"

Joshua explained her connection to the organized crime family while Kaylee resumed her pacing, her phone clutched in her hand. His heart hurt for her and all he could do was pray that whoever had taken Duncan had done it because they wanted him. Not because they wanted to hurt Kaylee.

Clay blew out a low breath. "All right. I'll talk to the special agent in charge here. His name is Henry Gilstrap. We're good friends and have worked together before. I'll see what he thinks about this latest bit of information."

While Clay stepped away to find his friend, Joshua went to Kaylee and took her cold hands in his. She looked up at him, tears swimming in her eyes. His heart nosedived and, with a groan, he pulled her to him. "I'm sorry, Kaylee. We'll find him. We will."

"What if we don't? I simply don't think I could stand it, Joshua. I didn't know it was possible to love a child so much in such a short time, but I do and—"

He tilted her face to his. "We have to find him. We *will* find him." The hoarse desperation in his voice took him by surprise. Apparently, he'd learned to love a child in a very short time, as well.

The thought scared him to death.

Clay came back, the frown on his face not encouraging. He planted his hands on his hips. "Kaylee, I've got to say, we're confused."

"What? Why?"

"The alarm system is intact and working fine. No one entered or exited the house through the doors or windows. No wires are cut, nothing. The one thing that kind of puzzles us is that there are some footprints in the grass in the backyard that look like someone walked around out there."

"So, what does that mean?"

"I'm not sure yet. We're going to get a cast of one of the prints and see what Forensics comes up with. Could be nothing, but at least we'll have it just in case."

Clay jerked his head at Joshua indicating he'd like to speak with him privately. Joshua raised a brow, but nodded. "Hey, do you have any water bottles?" he asked her.

"Um, yes, I think so." She wiped a stray tear. "Or I can make some more coffee." She looked around. "Looks like we might need it."

"That's a good idea."

She headed for the kitchen and Joshua turned to Clay. "What is it you want to say that you don't want Kaylee to hear?"

Clay sighed. "I hate to even bring the possibility up, but feel I have to. Could she have done this? Done something with Duncan? Could she have, ah, hurt him and then…" He shook his head. "We've got officers searching Dumpsters and every nook and cranny up this street and down the next, but I gotta tell you, I'm having a hard time wrapping my head around the idea she could have done something like that."

Shock rendered Joshua motionless for about two

seconds then he narrowed his eyes. "No way. Absolutely not."

Clay's shoulders relaxed a fraction. "You're awfully sure of that."

"Yes, I am. Clay, we were watching the place the whole time. No one left and no one entered."

"Then where's the baby?"

ELEVEN

The men stopped talking the minute she entered the room and Kaylee had the uncomfortable feeling that they'd been discussing her—and not in a favorable light. However, they didn't say anything, just took the bottles of water with thanks. "Coffee will be ready shortly."

"The guys will appreciate it," Clay said. He nodded to Joshua. "I'm going to get an update. I'll keep you in the know."

"Thank you," Kaylee said. She stopped and stared at the two animals resting in the corner of the kitchen by the pantry.

"What is it?" Joshua asked.

"The dogs didn't bark."

"What?"

"Whoever came in here and took Duncan didn't alarm the dogs. They didn't bark. Not even a growl."

He frowned. "So, they knew the person?"

"Maybe." She pressed her fingers against her eyes. "I still can't figure out how he got in. This makes no sense."

Deputy Logan Williams stepped into the den. "I think I know what happened—and if I'm right, the dogs wouldn't bark. They've been trained that whoever comes through that hall door attached to the medical building is a 'safe' person."

"What?"

"I was bashing myself about missing seeing whoever got in here, but… I think the person was already here."

Kaylee felt the blood drain from her face and swayed. Joshua gripped her upper arm and led her to a chair. To Logan, he said, "Explain that, will you?"

Clay joined them. "Yes, explain that, please."

"Follow me."

Logan led them, as well as the two special agents, down the hall to the door that led to the doctor's office. The apartment and the office were connected by two doors separated by a short hallway. He stopped Kaylee from going too close, but pointed to the floor. "You know what that is?"

Kaylee frowned. "Is that dirt?"

"I think so. I've taken a sample of it and have it in an evidence bag to send to the lab. I've checked out the door itself and it looks like it was jimmied open with something. Did you check it before you went to bed?"

"Um. Yes, I'm sure I did." She paused, trying to think. "Maybe." She groaned. "I don't know. Duncan was screaming for a long time after Joshua left and when he fell asleep, I did, too. I'm sorry, I probably wasn't as careful as I should have been." And her son had paid for it. Self-recrimination nearly took her to her knees.

"Hey, don't beat yourself up," Clay said, "I know what it's like to have a newborn and the sheer exhaustion that comes with them." He sighed. "But I hate to tell you this…"

"Tell me what, Logan?"

"You have a state-of-the-art alarm system, but this door isn't armed."

"What?" Joshua spat the word. "Why not?"

Clay shook his head. "I didn't even think about this door being a possible point of access."

"But it doesn't really matter," Kaylee said, "because every other door is. How would anyone get *in* to get to *that* door?" She jabbed a finger at it.

"During all the commotion of moving you in," Joshua said quietly. "The person slipped in and simply waited. When everything settled down and it was likely you and Duncan were sleeping, they simply opened the door, walked in and grabbed him."

"But the person still had to get out," she said, on the verge of tears once again. "The alarm never went off."

Joshua closed his eyes and groaned. "Yes, it did."

"When I threw open the front door," she whispered. "And whoever had Duncan could have just walked out the door at the back."

Clay slapped his notebook shut. "I would say that's probably what happened, but we've got the crime scene unit on the way and they'll see if they can get some prints. If it went down the way you just described, then the person had to have a car waiting somewhere. I'll start trying to find someone who was awake and either watching the street or working somewhere nearby."

"I don't believe this," Kaylee said. "I don't believe this!" Her knees gave out and if Joshua hadn't caught her, she would have landed on the floor.

"Come on, Kaylee. Let's go sit down."

She heard his words in some part of her brain and let him lead her into the living area where he pulled her down onto the couch. She turned into him, buried her face in his chest and let the sobs come.

* * *

At some point Kaylee had dropped into an exhausted sleep. With tears still drying on her cheeks, Joshua eased her onto the couch and tucked a pillow under her head. He covered her with the blanket from the back of the couch then leaned back, head against the cushion while he stared at the ceiling.

Trying to process the fact that Duncan was gone simply shattered him. He knew the chances of getting him back were slim, but going down that path of thought wouldn't be productive.

And that's what he needed to be right now. Productive. But how?

It wasn't like he was a cop and could do any actual investigation. He'd have to leave that to Clay and the others who'd taken over the kitchen.

But he could do something.

Glancing down at the sleeping woman, he decided he could help keep Kaylee calm, listen to her voice her grief, and hold her when she needed to cry.

And yet his brain wouldn't shut off. It didn't make sense. If it was her stalker, why break into the house and steal the baby when, up to this point, his entire focus had been on Kaylee?

Such as the man in the vehicle who'd tried to grab her the day he'd driven into town. And the shooting at the hospital. There appeared to be two different people after Kaylee. Were they working together? If the stalker wanted her alive, why take shots at her? If someone wanted the baby, why risk his life with a possible stray bullet? If it wasn't the stalker, but the other guy, the fact that he'd shot at her indicated he wanted her dead. So, the stalker and the shooter couldn't be working together, right?

So, who would want Kaylee dead and the baby alive? The only thing that made sense was her stalker and possibly the Rosetti family. Regardless of what Kaylee said, Joshua didn't see them being okay with never seeing the child who was their grandchild and nephew.

Clay would be checking on that, no doubt. Or the team in the kitchen would.

His head began to pound.

When the dogs wandered into the living room and settled themselves on the floor in front of the mantel, Joshua decided he'd call Natalie to come stay with Kaylee. He had to get going to make sure everything was okay at the clinic.

He picked up Kaylee's phone and swiped it, frowning when he saw it wasn't password protected. Not exactly a great idea, but for now, he was glad. He found Natalie's number and sent her a text explaining Duncan's kidnapping and asked if she could spend the rest of the night with Kaylee.

She wouldn't be alone with all of the feds in the kitchen, but he figured she might appreciate someone else in the house who would offer her support. Kaylee's father and his mother needed to be told what had happened. He dialed Kaylee's father's number. The man answered on the second ring. "Hello?" The raspiness in his voice said Joshua had woke him up. "Hi, Mr. Martin."

"Joshua? Is everything okay?"

"No, sir, not really." He told the man what had happened.

"I'll be there in a few minutes."

"No. I...didn't tell Kaylee I was calling. I just wanted you to know. I mean, Duncan *is* your grandson."

"Thank you. Please let me know if there's anything I can do to help."

"You can let my mother know."

Kaylee's phone buzzed and he looked at the screen. Natalie.

"I'll call Olivia. She may want to come right over."

"Just hold off on that right now if you don't mind."

A pause. "All right. Call us when Kaylee's ready."

"Thanks."

Natalie's text said she would be right over.

Ten minutes later, Joshua opened the door before she could knock. "Thanks for coming," he said softly.

"What happened to Duncan? Where is he?"

Joshua led her into the kitchen where he found one unoccupied chair. Her wide eyes took in the scene as she settled herself in the seat. He poured them both a cup of coffee. Someone had made a fresh pot. Probably one of the agents.

Once Natalie had her hands wrapped around the cup, Joshua explained.

"I don't believe this," she said. "Who could have taken him? And why?"

"We don't know. Trust me, if we did, we wouldn't be here."

"Of course." She ran a shaky hand over her blond hair. "You care about her a lot, don't you?"

Heat built in his cheeks. "I do care about her. And Duncan. I'm sick that I let this happen."

"I'm pretty sure you're not to blame."

"Maybe not, but…"

"But you'll be there for her when she needs someone. Because her father sure won't be."

Joshua wasn't so sure about that, but kept his mouth shut on that topic. "I'll be there for her. Whatever she needs, but she's going to need more than me."

Natalie nodded. "I can stay with her the rest of tonight, but I've got to be in court in the morning. I mean, I guess I can figure something out. Yes, I should do that. I'll call my boss and—"

Joshua reached out and squeezed her hand, and she snapped her lips shut. He smiled. "It's okay. You don't have to cancel or change anything. My mother can come stay with her if need be."

"I don't need anyone to stay with me."

Joshua jerked around at the sound of Kaylee's voice behind him. "Hey."

"Hey."

"We didn't mean to wake you."

"You didn't. Any news?"

The desperate hope in her voice nearly killed him. "No. But it's an all-out hunt. Everyone is searching."

Special Agent Mike James approached. "We might have something," he said to Kaylee.

"What?"

"We found a guy who says he might have seen someone leaving the premises with a baby."

Kaylee stepped forward. "Who? When? Where is this guy?"

"We're questioning him outside. But he may not be very reliable. He's twitchy and smells like alcohol. Says he doesn't want to talk to the cops, but that he'll talk to you."

"Me? Well, unreliable is better than nothing," Kaylee said. "What's his name?"

"Walter Morgan."

Joshua's heart sank.

"Oh," Kaylee said. Then, with a quick nod, she headed for the door. "I'll talk to him."

Kaylee hurried toward the police cruiser where Clay had Walter in the back seat. The man had a bottle of water his right hand and a carton of fries propped between his knees. Clay met her gaze and gave her a rueful smile. "He wanted food before he'd talk."

She nodded and slid in next to the man. "Hi, Walter."

"Hi," he mumbled around a mouthful of fries. "I would have told you what I saw without the food."

"I know." Heart thundering in her chest, she waited.

He swallowed. "I was sitting out on the front porch of the B and B when I heard the alarm go off at the doc's office. I started walking this way when this lady comes hurrying out of your place. She was holding something against her chest like this." He held his hands to his chest in the way someone would hold a baby against themselves.

"Wait a minute," Clay said, "it was a woman?"

"I think so. She was small with something covering her hair. Like a scarf or something. I couldn't see her face since she was moving sideways to me." He gestured to his profile. "You know, like this."

"Right." A woman. Kaylee's first thought went to Misty, the woman who'd lost her baby. Immediate guilt assaulted her. Just because the woman was grieving her dead baby didn't mean she'd taken Duncan. "Anything else?"

He stuffed another couple of fries into his mouth and shook his head.

"Okay, thanks, Walter."

"Yep. Hope you find him." His eyes met hers. "I'm really sorry. If I had known what was happening, I would have tried to stop her."

"No, it's probably best you didn't. She could have had a gun or something."

He nodded and finished off the fries. "Can I go now?"

Kaylee looked up at Clay who'd been listening to the exchange. Clay nodded and Walter slipped out the other door and headed back to the B and B.

Kaylee climbed out of the cruiser and crossed her arms, suddenly chilled to the bone in the cold night air.

A coat dropped across her shoulders and she turned to see Joshua. He was still there. She cleared her throat. "I don't want to think it's true, but I believe you need to check Misty Randall's house. She was here earlier, watching Duncan sleep and grieving deeply the loss of her own baby."

Clay raised a brow. "All right. We'll head over there now."

Special Agent Henry Gilstrap stood to the side. Kaylee hadn't even noticed him earlier, but he nodded. "I'll go with you."

"You'll let me handle this?" Clay said. "She's a mother whose baby died a couple of weeks ago."

"You can handle it," the agent said. "I'll be there for backup should you need it."

Clay nodded.

"I want to come, too," Kaylee said. "If she's got him, it may take a mother-to-mother heart-to-heart. You know what I mean?"

At first, Clay hesitated, then nodded. "All right, but you'll stay in the car until we need you. If we need you."

"Fine." She wasn't about to argue, she just wanted to be there. Not pacing the floor of her den, waiting on the phone call. She looked at Joshua. "Will you come, too?"

He gripped her fingers. "Of course."

Within minutes, they were in the police cruiser and headed toward the woman's home. Special Agent Gilstrap rode in the front passenger seat. Joshua sat next to her in the back and she was extremely glad for his presence.

The headlights cut through the dark and Kaylee's arms ached to hold her baby again. She whispered prayers, believing they were heard, but with the understanding that just because she wanted the prayers answered in a specific way didn't mean it would happen.

Hadn't she prayed that God would change Tony's heart? That he would realize his love for her and for Duncan? Hadn't she prayed day in and day out for that?

Her throat tightened. She'd lost so much. First her mother. Then her father had withdrawn almost completely from her life. Then Tony had cheated on her and kicked her out of her home.

Sobs wanted to break through. She couldn't lose Duncan, too.

A muscled arm slid around her shoulders and she found herself once more snuggled up against Joshua.

What was it about him? How was he so in tune to her feelings that he knew what she needed? And why was he so willing to give it to her?

"He's going to be fine. We're going to find him," he whispered against her cheek.

"I know." Staying positive and believing he was right was the only way she was going to survive this.

Clay slowed, and Kaylee's tension rose with each passing second. He finally stopped and she stared the small, cute house. Was her baby inside?

"Stay here," Clay said. "I'm going to go talk to her." He flicked a glance at Special Agent Gilstrap. "Misty knows me. Let me talk to her alone at first. I'll let you know if I need backup."

The agent nodded his assent. "I'll be here. Just wave if you need me."

Kaylee gripped Joshua's hand and kept her eyes glued to Clay's back as he walked up the three steps to the front porch.

The car's headlights illuminate the area and Kaylee had a good view.

The door opened and Misty stood there, clutching her robe around her.

Kaylee lowered the window.

"What's going on?" Misty asked.

"Someone broke into Kaylee's home tonight and took Duncan. Would it be all right if I come inside and ask you a few questions?"

"What?" The woman blinked, her eyes owlish and sleepy. "Took Duncan? Kaylee's baby?"

"Yes."

"But. Why?"

"That's what we're trying to figure out." Clay took his hat off. "Do you mind if I come in?"

"No, I guess not. Rick's working the night shift, so it's just me here."

Clay stepped inside the home and the storm door shut behind him.

"He's not here," Kaylee said softly.

"How do you know?"

"She wouldn't have let him in so easily."

"You never know."

She shot him a sad look, wishing she could believe that. "Yes," she said softly, "sometimes you *do* know."

TWELVE

Joshua hated that Kaylee had been right, but Clay had walked out of the house, shoulders slumped. Once behind the wheel of the cruiser, Clay turned sideways. "He's not there, Kaylee, I'm sorry. I searched every room and closet. Even went up into the attic. There's no clothes, no crib, nothing. There's absolutely no sign of a baby anywhere."

"She would have gotten rid of all of that. She wouldn't have wanted the reminder that her child wasn't..."

"Yeah."

Wasn't coming home. Joshua finished the sentence for her. And knew she was wondering if Duncan would be coming home.

He would be if Joshua had anything to do about it. "The next people to check with are the Rosettis."

Kaylee gasped. "What? You really think they could have done something like this?"

"Of course. You said yourself they're organized crime."

"Yes, but..." She shuddered. "I just...never saw that side of them, you know? They always seemed so normal. Whatever that means." She rubbed her eyes. "I guess what I'm saying is that if Tony hadn't told me their real business practices—or rather thrown it in my face when he was deep into his regrets about marrying me—then I never would have suspected."

"That's not surprising," Special Agent Gilstrap said from the front seat.

"One other consideration is that her stalker just wants the baby out of the way so he can have Kaylee to himself," Clay said.

The four of them fell silent. "No. He wouldn't do that," she said. And paused. "Would he?"

Unfortunately, Joshua didn't have an answer for her. From Clay's and the agent's lack of response, he figured neither of them wanted to be the one to answer that question. It was all speculation anyway.

"Let's get you home," Clay finally said. "Doors are still being knocked on. Security footage is being pulled from every camera on the street. Hopefully, we'll have something soon."

Kaylee drew in a shaky breath and Joshua's heart ached for her. For himself. He hugged her to him and she buried her face into his shoulder.

Clay cleared his throat. "I'm going to send someone out to the Rosettis' house to make sure Duncan isn't there."

"Don't call in advance," Joshua said, "they'll just hide him."

"Thanks for the advice, cuz. I never would have thought of that."

Joshua grimaced at the sarcasm. Okay, he'd take the hint and let Clay do his job.

"When will they go?" Kaylee asked, her voice low, hoarse.

"As soon as I can get someone out there."

Exhaustion swept him and Joshua leaned his head against the seat.

"When will we know something?" Kaylee asked. "When will someone call and tell you if Duncan is at the Rosettis'?"

"Probably within the next hour or so."

"Okay. An hour. I can wait an hour. Maybe."

But the time they reached her home, Joshua could tell her nerves were stretched just about as tight as he'd ever seen them. She climbed out of the back seat before he could offer to help her.

He followed at a slower pace while Clay and Special Agent Gilstrap discussed the visit to the home. He almost walked over to listen in, but noticed Kaylee standing frozen on the top step. "Kaylee?" A visible tremor racked her. He hurried over. "What is it?"

"It's… It…it's…his blanket." She reached for it.

Joshua clamped a hand over her wrist. "Don't. It's evidence. Clay?"

"Yeah?" He joined them on the porch. "What's that?"

"Duncan's blanket," she whispered. "And there's something wrapped in it." The stark fear in her voice grabbed Joshua by the throat. The little blue blanket was wrapped around the object neatly, specifically. With the ends tucked. Like someone would swaddle a newborn. Only the area where the baby's face would be was covered by a flap. And the blanket didn't move.

"Get back," Clay said. "Let me grab some gloves." Within seconds, he'd returned from the cruiser, snapping the gloves on.

"Duncan," she whispered. "My baby."

Joshua gripped her upper arms and pulled her to the side, then back down the steps. The door opened and

Special Agent Mike James stood there, hand on his weapon. "What's going on? Everything okay?"

"Not really," Clay said. "You didn't hear anything going on out here?"

"Nope, not a sound."

"And I called off outside patrols because there were two FBI agents in her kitchen. I'll beat myself up about that later." Clay held up a hand. "Don't move and don't touch anything."

The special agents frowned as Clay studied the small package. "Any wires?" Special Agent Gilstrap asked.

"Not that I can see."

Wires? Joshua's jaw tightened. A bomb? "No, he wouldn't use a bomb."

"What makes you say that?" Clay asked without looking away from the "gift."

"He wants her alive," Joshua said. "He wouldn't take a chance on killing her."

"Didn't seem to bother him when he was taking shots at her at the hospital."

Joshua frowned. "I know. That confuses me, but I'm still convinced he doesn't want to kill her."

Clay met his gaze. "Well, we're going to be careful anyway."

"Of course, but I'll be surprised if it's an explosive."

Special Agent Gilstrap nodded. "Get back." He looked up at the other agent. "Mike, you up to doing your thing?"

"I don't have a suit, but I can get closer to see if we've got a problem or not," the agent said. "Go on. Move back a little more."

No one hesitated.

Special Agent James pulled on his gloves and knelt. Once they were at a range he seemed comfortable with, he reached for the blue-wrapped bundle. With a steady hand, he pulled the top flap off and let it rest on the porch floor. "No wires so far." For the next few seconds, he continued his turtle-slow movements until the contents of the blanket were revealed. He looked up. "It's a baby doll. No indication of a bomb, but there's a note."

The breath whooshed from Kaylee's lungs and her grip on Joshua tightened. They moved in closer and Joshua could see the life-size baby doll. It had a note pinned to its little blue shirt.

"What does it say?" Kaylee asked. Her voice shook with a raw anger that took Joshua aback. Examining her face, he saw no fear, no backing down, just a steely determination.

The agent looked at Clay, who nodded. "'I know your arms feel empty, but soon that will change,'" he read. "'Because once we're together, your arms will never be empty again.'"

Kaylee shuddered, but the hard set to her face never wavered.

"Let me get an evidence bag," Clay said. "I'll send this off to Nashville. Maybe they'll find some prints or something."

"But we know who it is," Kaylee said.

"Yeah, and if he's arrested, you want enough evidence to put him back behind bars."

"Right."

Joshua sighed. "Let's get inside. Kaylee, you need to rest."

"As if."

"At least stretch out and close your eyes, even if you don't think you can sleep. You're going to need to be at your strongest while we're looking for Duncan.

You're not going to do him any good if you wear yourself down."

She bit her lip and nodded. "Fine. You're right. I
know you are. I just…"

"I know." He kissed her forehead, ignoring Clay's
raised brow.

They stepped inside the foyer of the small apartment
and the two agents returned to their seats at the table.
The phone sat front and center. He was skeptical that
the landline would ring if the kidnapper chose to call.
No, he'd call Kaylee's cell phone. Because Joshua had
no doubt the man had her number.

Kaylee alternated between staring at the phone on
her kitchen table, willing it to ring, and watching Clay
pace. She'd given up trying to sleep and knew she'd
regret it later, but for now, all she wanted was news
about Duncan.

Joshua leaned against the wall, hands shoved into
the front pocket of his khakis. He, too, looked ready to
explode with impatience and a desire to hear from the
officers in Nashville.

The minutes ticked on.

Finally, Clay's phone rang. He answered before it
fell quiet. "Starke here. Uh-huh. Right." A heavy sigh.
"Thanks. I'll pass that on to her."

But he didn't have to. Her heart had already fallen.

Joshua stepped over to her and gripped her shoulder.

Clay met her eyes. "Duncan's not there. There's no
sign of an infant."

A sob slipped out. She clapped a hand to her mouth,
rose and hurried into the den. She knew Joshua followed her and was glad to have his arms around her. It
helped, but the thought of never seeing her son again

sent pain shafting through her. Pain like she'd never before experienced and she wasn't sure how to process it.

Joshua let her cry without saying a word. When she finally could get a handle on herself, she looked up, saw the tears tracking his rugged cheeks and lost it again.

Minutes later, Joshua cleared his throat. "All right. I'm going to camp out here on your couch. Why don't you see if you can rest?" When she started to protest, he placed a finger over her lips. "I know. You won't be able to sleep. I get that. But at least try to rest. Duncan will need you when we find him."

"Yes. You're right. Okay."

He placed a kiss on her forehead and she stilled. "Kaylee…"

"Yes?" The odd look in his eyes stirred her curiosity.

"You're starting to consume my thoughts."

"Oh. Really? What do you mean?"

"You and Duncan are almost all I think about when I'm not with you." His lips tilted in that funny little quirk she'd just started noticing—and liking far too much. But his words filled her with dread.

"Okay. And that's bad. A distraction. I know." She picked at some imaginary lint on her pants.

"No. Yes. No."

"I'm glad you're so decisive about it."

A husky laugh escaped him and he ran a hand over his eyes before meeting her gaze again. "Yes, it's a distraction. I'm not sure it's bad, though."

"Explain?"

"All my life, I've been so focused on putting one foot in front of the other. Working hard to accomplish my dreams and be successful."

"And you've done a fabulous job."

"Yes, I have." No bragging, just fact. "But the past week or so with you and Duncan? It's started me thinking."

"About?"

He sighed and shook his head. "Everything but what I came home to think about."

"Stopping the wedding?"

"Yes." He raked a hand through his hair.

"Because you're with me." She stood. "Go home, Joshua." She knew her tone was cold and didn't care. If he was trying to find a way to excuse himself from her life, her problems, she'd make it easy for him. She wasn't the weak woman who'd begged her husband to let her stay. And she'd never be that woman again.

He snagged her hand. "No, Kaylee, that's not what I'm trying to say. I'm usually more articulate than this. What I'm trying to say is that I think my priorities may be changing."

"Oh." Embarrassed, she settled back onto the couch. "That's… I mean…ugh. I'm sorry."

"Don't apologize. I'm fumbling with my words. I guess what I'm saying is that since meeting you and Duncan—and seeing my mother with your father—my focus has changed. I'm…not so driven to stop the wedding."

"Really?"

"Yeah."

"Oh, good." She breathed a sigh of relief. "I'm glad."

He blinked. "You are?"

"Yes. I like your mom. She's been so sweet with helping. Not intrusive at all and just there if I need her." She dropped her gaze. "I'm ashamed, and I owe her an apology."

"I'm sure she understands."

"I know they're worried about Duncan." His name

came out on a sob and she bit her lip. "But they've been
so good about giving me—us—our space. If they want
to come wait with us for word on Duncan, I'm fine with
them coming over."

He nodded. "I'll call and tell them."

"Thanks."

He hesitated then kissed her forehead. "Kaylee, I
guess what I'm trying to say in my terribly inept way is
that you and Duncan have become extremely important
to me. I don't want to…" He blew out a breath. "Wow,
I can't believe how hard this is. I guess what I'm trying to say is…"

She pressed a finger against his lips. "You don't have
to say anything. Finding Duncan comes first. We can
talk about us later."

Us? Yes.

She really wanted them to be an "us" but couldn't
process that further. She had to focus on getting Duncan back before she could even think about the possibility of a romance with Joshua.

With more tears threatening, she squeezed his fingers and headed for her bedroom. Joshua was right
about one thing. She needed to rest so she could think.
Because she was going to figure out who had taken
Duncan and when she found that woman, Kaylee was
going to make sure she spent the rest of her life behind bars.

Once in her newly assembled bedroom, she ignored
the boxes that still needed to be unpacked and threw
herself across the bed. She clutched a pillow to her
stomach and let the tears flow once again.

Oh, please, God, bring my baby boy home.

Joshua finished the calls that he'd promised to make
and both his mother and Kaylee's father said they were

on the way. He went back into the kitchen to let the agents know and found them sitting in front of their computer, discussing the background of Kaylee's deceased husband. Clay leaned against the sink, sipping a cup of coffee.

Special Agent Gilstrap lifted his gaze from the computer screen. "She okay?"

"About as okay as one can expect in this situation."

"Right."

"Any news?"

The agent shook his head. "You would've heard it if there was."

"Of course. Thank you." Joshua looked at Clay. "Are you planning to stay here till morning?"

"I am. You?"

"Yes."

Clay nodded, the pensive look on his face raising Joshua's brow. "What are you thinking?" he asked.

"Just speculation."

"About?"

"I'm not sure I'm entirely comfortable letting the Rosetti family off the hook that easy."

"What do you mean?"

Clay pursed his lips then looked at the agents. "Kaylee said the family was organized crime, right?"

Joshua nodded.

"And while there's no evidence leading them to Duncan's kidnapping, I think we should check to see if there's any connection between them and Misty Randall."

Special Agent Gilstrap hesitated. "What are you thinking?"

Clay sighed. "I'm probably trying to connect dots that don't exist. Grasping at straws. But why not? We've got nothing else, right?"

"Maybe." The man shrugged. "All right. We're just sitting here waiting for a ransom demand to come in. Wouldn't hurt to start checking for connections. Tell me the names of the family members again."

"I know her husband was Tony, probably Anthony," Joshua said.

"That's all I need. I can find the rest of them. What about the woman you suspected? Misty?"

"Randall," Clay said.

Joshua waited while the man started typing. "But I thought you cleared her."

"I did." Clay set his mug on the counter. "But she's really the most likely suspect. She was here earlier in the day. She's a local, so she'd know that door wasn't armed." He shrugged. "Just makes sense."

"But there was no baby at her house or their house. No sign of one."

"True, but that doesn't mean anything. They might be keeping him somewhere else. Hiding him until everything blows over."

After a few seconds, Special Agent Gilstrap looked up. "Nothing. Misty's clean. Still working on Rosetti."

"Add Patrick Talbot into the mix," Clay said.

"What are you thinking?" Joshua asked.

"Let's focus on what we know. Talbot wants Kaylee, but he might not have wanted the baby. Maybe the shooting at the hospital was intended to kill Duncan."

Joshua shuddered. "That's beyond awful. Too terrible to even think about."

"I agree, but it seems plausible. The bullets never came close to Kaylee, did they?"

Joshua thought back to the shooting. The first bullet had hit the concrete near his feet. Not anywhere near Kaylee. "You're right, they didn't."

"So, if Duncan's out of the picture, that leaves Kaylee a single, childless woman. He may have figured without Duncan, Kaylee may even come to rely on him for comfort or support. He could console her, et cetera. You know what I mean."

"I don't know. Sounds like he wants to kill her more than keep her," Joshua muttered.

"Who knows what he really wants," Clay said. "He probably belonged in a heavily secured psychiatric hospital, but passed all the tests." He shrugged. "He knew all the right answers. Doesn't mean he's in touch with reality."

"Or he's just evil," Joshua said. "Could be he feels entitled to have what he wants and when he doesn't get it, he justifies going after it by whatever means possible. Including kidnapping."

"And attempted murder," Special Agent Gilstrap said. "If he's taking shots at you or the baby."

"And that."

Special Agent Gilstrap looked at his partner. "Let's keep working this angle. Can't hurt."

"I agree," his partner said.

Joshua pinched the bridge of his nose. "Then again, you've got to take into account the guy that tried to take her the day she had Duncan. That wasn't Talbot."

"Could be just a guy Talbot hired to grab her for him," Clay said.

"I don't think so, but I'm not sure why I don't think so. It's like mixed messages." He shook his head. "I'm exhausted. I'm going to crash on the couch for the next couple of hours. And then I'm going to have to head to the clinic."

"You're going to try and work?"

"There are patients who need to be seen."

"Not by you," Clay said. "Put a note on the door that all emergencies are to be handled by calling 9-1-1. I'll let dispatch know that if they need a doctor for an emergency they can call me and I'll get in touch with you. If you leave your number, you'll get every call from a toothache to a sprained ankle."

Joshua considered it. The man may be right. He'd done a lot of sleepless nights while in med school, of course, but the truth of the matter was, he didn't want to leave Kaylee. But he couldn't shirk his responsibility to the clinic, either. He respected Doc Anderson too much for that. "I'll call the doc first thing in the morning and see what he says."

Clay clapped him on the shoulder. "Up to you, man. I'm going to run home, make sure Sabrina and the kids are okay and snag a couple of hours of sleep. I'll have my cell phone on if you need me." The two agents would take turns sleeping as long as things were quiet.

They left the kitchen. Fatigue pulled at Joshua along with the worry for Duncan and Kaylee.

Please, God, let us find Duncan. Bring him back to us.

THIRTEEN

Kaylee rolled over two hours later, unsure what had awakened her. Something, though. Duncan? She gasped and shot out of bed, stumbling over the shoes she'd left on the floor. At his bassinet, she looked down and let out a low cry.

It was still empty.

Of course it was. This wasn't a nightmare she could just wake up from. Her baby was missing. Had been *stolen*.

But by who?

The sound near her window came again. She flinched. The curtains were drawn, so seeing what was making the noise wasn't possible.

She turned toward the door to let someone know when her cell phone vibrated, signaling a text message. She snatched it from the nightstand, but didn't recognize the number.

I know you're awake. I can see you.

Kaylee froze. Then shuddered. Another glance at the drape-covered window assured her that no one could see her.

Answer me. I know where Duncan is.

She caught her breath and let her fingers tap the screen.

Where is he?

Open the window.

Um. No. She hurried toward the door with every intention of letting the agents know Patrick was outside when her phone buzzed again.

If you don't open the window now, Duncan dies.

A picture of her baby popped up and she barely held back her scream. She froze, her hand reaching for the knob.

I really can see you. Come back to the window.

How could he see her? Probably some military night-vision binoculars or something. Something that sought a heat source. Such as her.

She hesitated then walked over to the window, her pulse pounding, her mouth dry with fear. And hope.

Parting the curtains, she came face-to-face with the man who played a prominent role in her recurring nightmares.

Patrick Talbot.

Fury mingled with fear. Instantly, she knew what was going to happen. He was going to make her go with him. But she couldn't be stupid. Then again, she couldn't give up this chance to get Duncan back.

Her fingers clutched her phone. She had to signal Joshua, but how?

Patrick had cut a hole in the window. Which explained why the alarm hadn't gone off. He'd planned this well. She marched over to him. "Where's my baby?"

A sly grin curved his lips and she wanted to retch.

"He's in a safe place," Patrick said, "but he's all alone and missing his mama, I'm sure. Come on and you can see him. Alert anyone that I'm here and he dies. It's really that simple."

"I thought you said he was alone."

"He is, but hidden very well. If I get caught, he simply starves to death—or freezes to death. Whichever comes first. But he *will* die if I get caught. Understand?"

Heart in her throat, she gave a slow nod.

"Now, come with me, Kaylee." He held up a pair of binoculars. Kaylee didn't know what kind they were, but understood they allowed him to see heat signatures through walls. "You know how to get out without setting off the alarm. The doctor's office is on a separate system. Go over there, turn it off and walk outside. Meet me at the blue SUV parked in front of the general store. Do you have your phone?"

"Yes."

"Call this number." He gave it to her and she dialed it with shaky fingers.

Was she really going to do this?

Did she have a choice?

He glanced at his device and nodded. "Good. Now I can hear everything you say."

"You didn't take his pacifier."

"What?"

She glanced behind her at the bassinet. "I want to get his pacifier. He might need it."

"He has one."

"Not his favorite. You left it when you took him. I don't want you to wonder what I'm doing when I reach into the bassinet."

"I didn't—" He gave a low, frustrated sound. "Fine, get it."

Kaylee thought fast. He was going to make her give up her phone as soon as she was in the car. "I need to get my shoes, too."

"Get what you want and come on! I'll be waiting and watching—" he shook the binoculars at her then held up his cell phone "—and listening."

The tightly leashed fury in his voice had her moving. She grabbed Duncan's pacifier from the bassinet and hurried to the door. Then paused. No, she needed to signal someone. She needed help, but how? Duncan's sweet face filled her mind and she drew in a deep breath.

The knock on the door startled her. She froze for a split second. "Kaylee? You awake?"

She opened her mouth then shut it.

"Answer him," Patrick hissed from the hole in the glass. "Get rid of him. Remember, Duncan's counting on you." Heart pounding, Kaylee crossed the room and opened the door. She bit her lip so she wouldn't blurt out the fact that Patrick Talbot was hiding outside her bedroom window.

Duncan. Remember Duncan.

Joshua's gaze met hers. "I just talked to Mom. She's beside herself and wants to be here for you if you want her to."

"Oh, Joshua, I just want my baby back."

"I know." He reached for her and she let him hold her. Just one more time. Words of comfort spilled from his lips, but she just relished his embrace while frantically trying to figure out how she was going to let him know what was going on.

"Come here."

"What?"

"Let's talk."

Uh-oh. "I really don't feel like talking right now."

"At least get some warm tea."

Anxious to get out the door, she nodded. "All right."

She followed him down the hall into the kitchen. The door on the opposite end of her den called to her. Fortunately, her jacket hung over the back of the recliner. She could grab it on her way out.

Duncan. *Mommy's coming, honey.*

Special Agent Gilstrap looked up. His partner wasn't in sight, but his phone rested beside the laptop. She looked at Joshua. "I'll just make some tea and head back to my room."

"I'll get it for you."

"All right. Thanks."

While Joshua moved to fix the tea, Kaylee edged to the table and let her hand hover over the other agent's phone. Could she? Did she dare? Would they realize it?

Probably.

Joshua said something and when Special Agent Gilstrap turned to respond, Kaylee slid the phone from the table. She sat in the empty chair and slipped the device into her shoe.

She took her tea from Joshua and sipped it. The warmth of the brew slid down her throat. "Thank you."

She rose, the cell phone in her shoe giving her comfort. And, hopefully, not a false sense of comfort. A hope that this would end well. "I'll see you in a bit."

Leaving the kitchen, she turned as though to head back to her bedroom. When the men started talking, she did a one-eighty to the opposite end of the hall, staying against the wall and out of their line of sight.

She grabbed her jacket from the recliner. Two more steps and she was at the door. She turned the lock, stepped through and shut the door quietly behind her. She hurried through the small hall, ignoring the fact that her baby's kidnapper had used this very same little area to hide so she could escape with Duncan. She...not Patrick. So, Patrick had hired someone—a woman—to take Duncan? But...why?

To get to Kaylee, no doubt. To use the baby just like he was doing.

And it was working.

Had the woman known the layout of the medical office and Kaylee's apartment? Was it someone she knew?

Didn't have to be. Public records could reveal the blueprints. And a simple fishing statement to the right person in town about the passageway between the two would be enough to get a lot of people talking. It's not like it was a secret. No, anyone who did a little research could easily have found out everything they needed to know to enable them to break into her home. The thought sickened her. She should have been more careful.

Finally, she was in the medical office. Hesitating, she hurried to the supply cabinet and unlocked it. Slipping a scalpel into her pocket, she took a deep breath. At least she wouldn't be completely unarmed.

She went to the alarm and punched in the code to turn it off. When she opened the front door, she almost rearmed the system, then hesitated. Instead, she cracked the door so it was barely discernible, yet not fully connected with the alarm sensor.

She hated to leave it open with all of the drugs in the

office, but they were behind a locked door in a locked cabinet. She'd take the chance if it meant possibly saving her life.

Kaylee spotted the blue SUV sitting exactly where Patrick had said it would be. With a deep breath and an urgent prayer, she walked toward it, praying she'd get to hold her son, but knowing Patrick wouldn't have brought Duncan with him.

Forcing one foot in the front of the other, she reached the vehicle. He was in the passenger seat. The windows were rolled down. "Get in, my love. It's time to fulfill our destiny."

The bad feeling in her gut churned into nausea. She fought it, gathered her strength and opened the driver's door. She slid into the seat and turned the key. She might be terrified out of her mind, but she was also determined to do whatever she had to do to bring Duncan home.

Joshua frowned when his phone vibrated once more. A message from the answering service. A patient needed him to call. But he'd passed his on-call responsibilities off to Melissa. He quickly forwarded the message to her and she acknowledged she'd take care of it.

Glad to have that off his plate, Joshua focused on something that had been bothering him for the past several days. He turned to Clay, who'd arrived a few minutes just after Kaylee had returned to her room. "I want to know how the guy who attempted to kidnap Kaylee on the day Duncan was born fits into the picture. Kaylee didn't recognize him. He wasn't her stalker. So... who was he? And why was he after her?"

Clay nodded and sipped at his fresh cup of coffee.

He'd brought them all a cup from the local diner. "I've thought about that, too."

"We got some security footage from the hospital on the shooter. Special Agent Gilstrap is running his face through NGI to see if a name pops up."

"NGI?" Joshua asked. He felt like he should know that, but the acronym escaped him.

"Next Generation Identification. One of the FBI's facial recognition programs. If the guy has a mug shot anywhere, the program will flag it. We'll get a galley of about twenty photos and, since you and Kaylee are the only ones who've seen the man, you'll have to manually go through each one to see if any of them are him."

"Okay. When will we have this galley?"

"Working on it," Special Agent Gilstrap said, his fingers flying over the keys of his laptop. His partner was moving stuff around, folders, equipment, his chair. Looking for something?

Joshua's phone buzzed once more before he could ask and he pulled it out to see what needed his attention so urgently. Only this time it wasn't about a patient. "The alarm on the medical office is indicating a problem. Looks like the front door is open."

Clay straightened. "I'll go check it out." He left, radio to his lips, speaking quickly as he walked through to the hall that would take him to the next building.

"Hey." Special Agent James threw up his hands. "I've been looking for my phone for the last ten minutes. Have any of you seen it? I know I left it right here when I walked the perimeter." He held up a black radio. "I had this, so I didn't bother carrying the phone. And now it's gotten up and walked off."

Joshua shook his head. "I haven't seen it. Sorry."

The special agent glared at his partner. "Gilstrap, are you messing with me? Because now's not the time."

"No, man. I don't play those games when we're on a case, you know that."

"Yeah, I do. So, where did the phone go?"

Joshua stared at the table where the agent pointed. "I saw your phone sitting there when Kaylee and I walked in earlier to get her some tea."

"And you didn't pick it up?"

"Of course not."

"Would Kaylee?"

"No, why would she?"

Special Agent James sighed. "You mind asking her if she saw it?"

"Of course not. I doubt she's sleeping." Joshua stepped into the hallway at the same time Clay returned from the medical clinic.

The tight look on the man's face had Joshua tensing. "What is it?"

"The front door to the clinic wasn't completely shut and the alarm system was turned off."

"What?" Joshua's head started to pound. "What's going on? There are only a few people who have that code."

"Did she have it?" Special Agent James asked from the hall entrance.

"I haven't checked yet." He wanted to stomp over to Kaylee's door, but forced himself to walk softly. He rapped on her door.

No answer.

"Kaylee?"

Had she fallen asleep?

He tried the knob and found it unlocked. Peering around the edge of the door, he scanned the room. Empty. "Kaylee?"

He strode to the window and shoved back the curtains. The hole in the glass stared back at him.

FOURTEEN

Kaylee's fingers flexed on the steering wheel. When she'd climbed into the driver's seat, he'd held his hand out for her phone then tossed it out the window. For the past ten minutes, they'd ridden in silence. "Where am I going?"

"Just keep driving. I'll tell you when to turn."

"But Duncan's okay?"

"He will be as long as you behave yourself."

"Just tell me where he is, please." The desperate need to know drove every other thought from her mind.

"I can see I made the right decision. At first, I wanted Duncan, too, but it's obvious that he would be too great a distraction for you."

"A distraction? I'm his *mother*!"

"Having a mother is overrated. I didn't have one."

"Right. And you turned out so well."

His fist connected with her cheek and she cried out. Her head cracked against the window. He grabbed the wheel and managed to keep them from tumbling down the embankment into the trees.

Lights flashed behind her eyes. She groaned and slammed on the brakes. The SUV skid to the side and she came to a stop on the shoulder.

"Don't provoke me, Kaylee. Now apologize."

She grit her teeth and took inventory. Decided nothing was broken, but she was going to have a whopper of a bruise and probably a headache for a couple of days. "I'm sorry."

"I'm not sure how sincere that is, but for now, I'll accept it."

Kaylee realized her shoe with the phone had slipped off during the incident and she swallowed. Where was it?

Gingerly, she shifted her socked foot, trying to locate the device. "Get out," he said.

"What?"

"Get out. I'm going to take us the rest of the way."

Oh, no. No, no, no. He'd find the phone. "My shoe came off. I need to put it back on."

"So, put it back on and when I get out, you slide over. Understand? And if you run, Duncan dies. I'm tired and I'm ready for this to be done."

His words chilled her. "Are you going to kill me?"

He shot her a sideways look. "Of course not. We're going to have a wonderful life together. But I know it's going to take some time to convince you of that."

"So, what do you have planned?"

"You'll find out soon enough."

"But I'll be with Duncan, right?"

"Of course. Now, let's go."

Kaylee reached down and found her shoe, but couldn't find the phone. He'd already rounded the front of the vehicle and opened the driver's door. "Move over. Now."

Panicked, the phone her only hope of rescue, she bit her lip, slipped her shoe on and just prayed that if she couldn't see the phone, he couldn't, either.

He slid behind the wheel with a glare. She kept her

mouth shut. Once they were moving again, he slapped a fist against the wheel. "Why did you reject me, Kaylee?"

"Reject you? How did I reject you? I didn't know who you were."

"Exactly. I came into your ER a broken man and you patched me right up. You offered me words of comfort, your voice touched something in my soul, but I was just a case for you, wasn't I? Even though you told me how glad you were that I'd survived and how God must have been looking over me and that he had a purpose for me."

"I remember that."

He blinked. "You do?"

"Of course."

He'd been in a rather serious car accident, emerging with a broken wrist and a fractured ankle. But other than that, he'd been fortunate. The car he'd collided with had been totaled, killing the three people in it. Patrick had been cleared of any wrongdoing, the toxicology report on the driver of the other car had indicated an elevated blood alcohol level.

"And, Patrick, I was very glad you'd lived, but I was glad in a way that any decent person would be to hear a drunk driver hadn't taken out yet another innocent victim. Why would you think you were more? We'd never met before that night."

"But we connected. You cared." He paused. "At least, you seemed to. But it was all a lie, wasn't it?"

"No! None of it was a lie. Of course, I cared. I cared about you like I would any human being who was hurting."

"We connected. You held my hand. You gave me such comfort that I knew we were meant to be together."

"So, you started sending me gifts." The memories of the multitude of roses, candy, stuffed animals and love letters made her shudder.

"But you didn't want me or my gifts. I was kind. I would have romanced you and made you happy. I gave you a choice. Now you will have no choice. You will be mine. We'll be together now. Like we were meant to be from the very moment we met."

He was certifiable. Out of touch with reality. "You really think this behavior is okay? That taking my child and kidnapping me is acceptable? Don't you understand that this is wrong?"

He slid her a glance. "You think I'm crazy, but I'm not," he said. "I know that society and the law frowns on what I'm doing. I know that if I get caught, I'll go to jail again. But it's simply that they don't understand the facts, they only look at things in black and white. They don't understand that people sometimes need their decisions made for them. Because they don't know what's best."

"Like me?"

"Yes." He sounded surprised she'd ask. Like she was confirming his beliefs instead of just asking a question. "Like you."

"So, why did you try to kill me at the hospital?"

He frowned. "What? I didn't."

"You shot at me."

"What are you talking about?"

Seriously? "The shooting at the hospital. Someone was shooting at me. If you had this in mind, if we were meant to be together, why would you try to kill me?"

"I didn't. I wouldn't."

"Well, someone did."

Kaylee saw his eyes narrow and his nostrils flare.

"It wasn't me."

"But you know who it was."

He fell silent, his jaw working. He was thinking hard about something.

"Who was it?" She pressed. "The guy who tried to kidnap me the day Duncan was born."

He turned at the light, anger rolling off him in waves.

Maybe she should have just kept quiet. "That same guy tried to kidnap me from the clinic."

"No," he whispered. "He wouldn't betray me like that."

"Who wouldn't, Patrick?"

"He said you would be mine. He wanted the baby, but you were mine."

Senses sharpening, she jerked another look at him. "What do you mean, Patrick? Who wanted the baby?"

"He tried to kidnap you?"

"Yes," she answered, hoping that he would simply start talking and clear up her confusion. With her fear under control at the moment, her brain was able to function. It was clear he was working with someone. But who?

"That wasn't the deal," he muttered. "That wasn't the deal."

She wanted to scream, to yell at him to explain, but was afraid that would shut him down completely.

His breathing huffed through his nose and his hands shook. He was mad, but not at her. "He lied." He slammed a fist on the steering wheel and let out a scream.

Kaylee jumped when he jerked the wheel in his fury. He corrected the vehicle and kept them on the road, but she wished she knew what he was thinking. Had she made a mistake? Had she just made him angrier by questioning him?

He wasn't angry; he was fuming. But not at her.

"What's that? What's on the floor?"

Her heart pounded. The phone. When he jerked the car, he must have dislodged it.

Still driving, he reached down and snagged it from

the floor. His fingers curled around the device and the wheel simultaneously. Then he shot her a hard look, rolled down the window and gave it a toss. Without saying a word, he rolled the window up and drove.

In silence.

Complete and utter silence.

Nausea threatened. That phone had been her only hope. The reason she hadn't lost her mind. Now she was on her own now with no hope of being tracked.

Thirty minutes later, after winding through the mountains on a single-lane road, he pulled into the drive of a small cabin. Heart pounding, she waited while he turned the vehicle off. Darkness covered them. "Is he in there?"

Patrick continued to mutter under his breath.

She touched his arm. "Patrick, is my baby in that cabin?"

He turned, with a snakelike quickness that had her backing up against the door, cringing at the thought of his hard fist lashing out again. Her face throbbed and her head pounded, but she'd take a beating if it meant finding her child.

Patrick shook his head. "He lied to me. I let them take the baby before I came for you because he said that was best. But he's setting me up, isn't he?"

Cold, stark terror hit Kaylee right in the chest. Patrick was very possibly suffering a severe form of paranoia.

And Duncan wasn't in that cabin.

If she allowed Patrick to get her in there, she had no doubt she'd never walk back out the door.

Joshua paced the hallway. "Where would she go? She can't have been gone that long. How would she get out without setting the alarm off?"

"Just like the kidnapper got in to take Duncan," Clay said.

Yeah, he knew that. "And she walked out the front door of the clinic. And no one saw her because we're all in here."

Clay rubbed his chin. "She was obviously coerced. She left the door cracked, hoping it would set off the alarm on your app."

Special Agent Gilstrap stepped into the kitchen. "We found her phone." He set it, bagged and tagged, on the table. "When she got in the vehicle, she was probably told to toss it."

The phone.

"Special Agent James, did you track down your phone?"

"I did."

"Where is it?"

The man motioned him over. "I think Kaylee picked it up. I'm watching it go down the interstate even as we speak."

"He's got her," Joshua said.

"Yeah, that's what I figured. I've got a chopper getting ready to head that way. They'll give us an idea of what we're dealing with."

Joshua raked a hand through his hair. "I know what we're dealing with. We've got to get there." He spun to Clay. "Can you drive us?"

"Yes, I was thinking the same thing."

"I've got local officers heading that way, as well," Special Agent James said. "I don't expect a call to come in, but I don't want to leave the phones unmanned. I'll stay here. If you need me, use the radio."

"Got it." Clay headed for the door with Joshua right

on his heels. "Update me on her location every few minutes."

"I'll have it sent to your phone so you can follow it yourself. No middleman needed."

Once they were in Clay's cruiser, with Special Agent Gilstrap behind them, they took off in the direction indicated by Special Agent James's phone.

Three minutes later, Clay's phone rang. He put it on speaker. "Yeah?"

"She's stopped moving."

"Where?"

Special Agent James gave him the location in longitude and latitude. At Clay's urging, Joshua punched it in the GPS on the dash. "Let the others know."

"Will do."

Clay hung up and pressed the gas.

Road lights flashed past Joshua. Faster than he'd ever gone before in a car. And he wanted to urge Clay faster still. Ten minutes later, they pulled to a stop. Clay spoke into his phone, which he had on speaker. "You're sure this is the right location?"

"That's what the tracker says."

More law enforcement pulled in behind them. "There's nothing here," Joshua said. "It's just an open road."

Clay and Joshua got out of the cruiser. Clay popped the trunk and removed a large light from a black bag. He flipped it on and the powerful beam lit up the night. Another officer did the same on the other side of the road. Joshua stayed with Clay as the man swept it back and forth around the area. They tromped through the trees, finding nothing at first, then something glinted in the last pass of the light.

"There," Joshua said, "near the edge of the road."

Clay hurried over. "It's a cell phone."

"Looks like Special Agent James's," Joshua said raking a hand through his hair. "I recognize the case. She's not here."

"He must have found the phone and made her ditch it."

Fear centered itself in his chest. "So, now what?"

Clay shook his head. "I don't know. They could be anywhere."

"Well, we can't just stand here doing nothing." Desperation clawed at him. "We have to keep looking!"

"Where? That phone was our only hope. We don't have a clue where they could have gone from here."

He was right. *Oh, Lord, please keep Kaylee and Duncan safe. And help us to find them!*

Kaylee wasn't sure how long they sat there. Patrick continued to rock, his gaze on the cabin, words too low and disjointed for her to catch. A light glowed from within, giving the cabin a deceptively homey appearance. Unfortunately, it was the only light she'd seen for the past several miles. Of course he would pick an out-of-the-way place to bring her.

Where no one could hear her scream.

Indecision warred while she waited him out. Everything in her cried out to find a way to escape. But how? Did she dare take the chance that Duncan wasn't inside the cabin? Patrick had said he'd allowed someone else to take him. And that person had been a woman, according to the eyewitness. But how reliable was the homeless Walter Morgan?

Please, God, she prayed, *tell me what to do.*

She waited, mind spinning, stomach churning. Something wasn't right. Other than the obvious. She glanced at Patrick from the corner of her eye. Still, he sat, mouth moving but no sound emerging. Should she say anything?

No, not while he was calm. She raised shaky fingers to touch her cheek and winced at the sharp stab of pain. She was going to have a whopper of a bruise, but she didn't think anything was broken.

Then he moved. "Get out." For a moment, she froze and he shoved her. "Go! You need to learn to do things the first time I tell you to, you understand?"

"Of course." She opened the door and slammed it, anger and fear boiling.

He climbed out on his side and shot her a warning glance. The gun glinted in the moonlight. How good of a marksman was he? He looked pretty comfortable holding the weapon, which made her think he might not be a bad shot.

He motioned with the gun. "Into the cabin."

She hesitated. "What's going to happen once I go inside? I want to see my baby."

"Well, unfortunately, that's not going to happen tonight, but if you're good and obey me, then you might get to see him tomorrow."

So, he wasn't in the cabin.

"Patrick, I need to know he's safe and warm and no harm is going to come to him before I set foot in there." She jabbed a finger at the cabin then planted her feet and curled her hands into fists at her sides.

"Get inside!" He didn't seem to know what to do with her refusal to move.

Kaylee swallowed, praying she wasn't pushing him too far. "Tell me where he is."

"He's fine, okay? He's safe in a warm bed. I'm not a monster. I wouldn't hurt a little baby." He walked toward her and jabbed the gun against her temple. "But I would hurt his mother. Now inside!"

Fear continued to climb within her. As well as relief. She prayed he wasn't lying to her about Duncan because she was going to have to act as though the baby was safe. She put one foot in front of the other as she scanned the area. Trees all around. Just on the other side of the car. But it was dark. And cold. Fortunately, she still had her jacket on. No gloves, but she had pockets.

If she ran, where would she go?

Did it matter? Three more steps and she'd be at the base of the front porch. A plan played out in her mind and she broke out in a cold sweat at the thought of doing it.

Two more steps.

One.

She placed a foot on the first step, then the next.

Patrick stayed behind her.

With a cry, she stumbled and went down, her leg swinging out behind her, catching him in the knee.

His yell blended with hers and he hit the concrete walkway, the gun spilling from his grip.

With no time to grab it, Kaylee leaped to her feet and took off for the woods behind the cabin.

"Kaylee! I'm coming for you! You just killed your son!"

She stumbled. Almost stopped. But it was too late. She'd infuriated him and knew he would probably kill her if he got his hands on her now. She ran, her sneakered feet pounding against the dense wood floor. Branches reached out to grab her, one scraped across her cheek and she cried out, but didn't stop.

She could hear him behind her, screaming at her to stop. "Even if you get away from me, you'll die from exposure. We're miles away from the nearest person. There's no cell reception up here. What do you think you're going to do? You need me!"

The darkness aided her, but the moon worked against her. A particularly dense cluster of trees jutted to her right. She went left, found a large oak and started climbing.

FIFTEEN

Joshua paced in front of the cruiser while the other officers continued to search the area. He felt like it was a futile effort, even as he knew they had to do it, but was racking his brain to find another way to figure out where Patrick Talbot would take Kaylee.

There had to be a way. Talbot had been thinking about it for a long time, had been planning what he would do when he got to her. So…what?

He walked over to Clay who'd just popped the trunk and tossed his flashlight into the black bag. "Who visited him in jail? Besides his lawyer, I mean."

Clay shut the trunk. "Why?"

"Because someone is helping him. And if he's got help, it stands to reason that someone would have visited him to set up this whole thing."

"Yes, once we decided there were two separate people involved, I checked into that."

"And?"

"The log showed that the only visitors he had were his two brothers, his mother and his pastor."

"And they all checked out?"

"All except one. Records show that he only has one brother, but the jail shows two brothers signing in. Officers are still trying to track down one of them and haven't found him yet. The two sisters and older brother all have alibis. And they seem to be upstanding citizens. One sister is a stay-at-home mother and her husband is a mechanic at a local garage. The other sister is a lawyer. And the brother is an accountant for a reputable firm about two hundred miles from here." Clay rubbed his eyes and motioned for Joshua to get in.

Joshua stilled. "Wait a minute," he said. "Kaylee said Talbot has two sisters and only *one* brother, not two, so I think you're on the right track. If you find out who the guy masquerading as Talbot's brother is, I think we'll have a lot of our questions answered."

Clay fastened his seat belt. "You got a look at the guy who tried to grab Kaylee, didn't you?"

"Yes, and it wasn't Talbot."

Clay pulled the laptop toward him. "Take a look at these pictures." He tapped the keyboard, clicked and tapped some more.

Photos loaded and Joshua leaned in. "Who are these guys?"

"The pictures NGI pulled up just a bit ago."

Joshua pointed. "Who's that?"

"Talbot's older brother."

"I don't recognize him."

Clay flipped to the next picture. "This is the other guy who signed the log. Younger brother."

"That's him!" Lowering his voice, Joshua said, "That's the guy who tried to snatch Kaylee when she was in labor."

"Seriously?"

"Dead serious."

"What's this guy's name?"'

"No idea. He signed the log and had ID as Randy

Talbot, but NGI says his real name is Randy Morris."
His fingers flew over the keyboard. "I'm sending his
information to Special Agent James with a request for
them to put a BOLO on him."

"What could his connection be to Kaylee?"

"I don't know." More key tapping. "Could be someone hired him."

"Yeah…but who?"

"Maybe Talbot. Hired him to help him escape the
work detail and then to kidnap Kaylee and bring her
to him?"

"It's a logical theory."

Logical, but was it the right one?

Joshua's phone rang. He didn't recognize the number, but answered anyway just on the off chance it was
Talbot—or Talbot letting Kaylee call. Heart pounding,
he prayed to hear Kaylee's voice. "Hello?"

A throat cleared. "Um. This the doc?"

His heart sank and he pressed fingers to burning
eyes. "Yes. Is this Mr. Morgan?"

"Walter."

"I'm kind of in the middle of something, Walter.
Could I call you back in a little bit?"

"You looking for Kaylee?"

Joshua sat straighter, his attention now hyper-focused
on the call. "I am. Why?"

"Saw all the commotion over at her house. I also
saw her get in the SUV with that guy snooping around
her window."

"Wait a minute. What guy?"

"I don't know who he was. I saw them talking at the
window to her bedroom. Kaylee didn't look happy, but
she finally shut the curtains and the guy walked back
to his SUV. I was going to let someone know, but then

a few minutes later, Kaylee came out of the house and rushed to get in the driver's seat. I thought everything was okay, but still had a funny feeling in my gut. So, I followed 'em."

Joshua blinked. "You did? How?"

"On my scooter. Tried to call, but didn't have a signal. Had to come back down the mountain a fair piece until I had a couple of bars. Something's not right. I don't think she should be with that guy. Not with her baby missing and all."

"You've got great instincts, Walter." Joshua motioned for Clay to start driving. "Tell me where they went."

"I would, but there's just one problem."

"What's that?"

"There's a bunch of twists and turns. I'm not sure I can find it again."

Kaylee huddled in the branches of the tree, shivering and praying. She ignored her protesting body. She still hadn't fully recovered from giving birth and now she was having to climb a tree to flee a killer. A sob built in the back of her throat but she swallowed it back and focused on survival.

From her position on a thick branch about nine feet off the ground, she had a pretty good view of the area beneath her, thanks to the moonlight. Footsteps hurried, twigs and other debris crunched under Patrick's feet.

Kaylee held her breath when he stopped right under her. She stayed still, praying he wouldn't look up. The glow of the cabin to her left, the vehicle through the woods to her right. The only way to call for help and get away from the person who wanted her dead.

With no idea where she was, she didn't dare try walking out. Not with the temperature dropping. And yet, she couldn't stay where she was.

Or could she?

Could she wait for Patrick to leave then sneak into the cabin? While she didn't hold out much hope for a landline telephone, it was possible.

"Kaylee! You have ten seconds to get over here. Or I let Duncan die."

So much for not being able to hurt a little baby. She shuddered. Desperation and indecision clawed at her. She couldn't go down. That wasn't an option.

Think, Kaylee!

Her heart pounded and she finally knew what she had to do. Patrick wasn't going to let her have Duncan regardless. Her only hope of saving her baby was in escaping the man who wanted to hold her captive—or most likely kill her when she didn't fall into line with his plans.

When ten seconds passed, he cursed and punched the trunk of the tree where she hid.

Finally, he stomped off, deeper into the woods and away from the cabin. She waited. Listening while her heart thudded in her chest. Her lungs were tight, in desperation of the deep breath she'd yet to take in fear that he'd somehow hear it. But now he was gone. Out of sight, out of hearing range. She hoped.

It was now or never.

Carefully, as quietly as possible, she lowered herself to the limb beneath. Only to feel hard fingers wrap around her ankle. A scream ripped from her throat and she jerked her leg. His fingers slipped. Another hard pull released his grip.

She scrambled to the branch above, clinging, her

mind grasping for an escape plan. "Stop this, Patrick! You can't just force someone to have a life with you!"

His dark eyes glittered up at her as he placed a hand on the branch that would bring him closer to her. "Then we'll just share death together."

She whimpered. *God, help me, please!*

Kaylee stood and grabbed the large branch at her waist and hefted herself onto it. The only way she was going to get away was to make *him* go away.

The plan in place, she waited, watching him while her heart beat at an explosive pace. "It's obvious we've got some work to do, Kaylee. In time you'll learn your place. You'll learn to obey me and earn my love."

"Or you'll kill me? Oh, yeah, that's real love." She sucked in a harsh breath. "You don't know what love is. Just go away and leave me alone. Please!"

"Can't do that. You were promised to me and I'm going to have you."

"Who promised you?"

He inched up. When his left hand reached for the next branch, Kaylee said a silent prayer and jumped.

Right onto the fingers holding the branch.

He let out a harsh yell and let go, cursing her even as he held his grip on the branch with his right hand.

"No," she whispered. "Let go." But he didn't. He was fighting hard to get a good grip. When his injured hand grasped the branch, his face appeared above it for a brief second. With one last, desperate cry, she held on tight and swung her foot, aiming for his face.

His nose crunched. Another cry ripped from him and this time he fell, bouncing and crashing through the tree...

...all the way to the ground.

He landed with a thud.

Kaylee waited, panting, heart in her throat. Patrick lay at the bottom of the tree, unmoving. But was it a trick? No, it couldn't be. He'd fallen a long way.

The seconds ticked past. Still, he didn't move. She lowered herself limb by limb until she reached the last one where she stayed motionless, hovering, watching. His chest rose and fell in a steady rhythm, but the gash on his head said he'd taken a hard knock. It wasn't a trick. She was safe for now. A sob rose in her throat and she swallowed it back.

From her perch on the last limb, Kaylee leaped to the ground and took off toward the cabin.

Please let there be a phone. Please let there be a phone.

Her chant became her prayer as she dodged limbs and did her best to avoid tripping on the undergrowth.

Finally, she broke through the tree line. The little cabin sat peacefully to her left. She dashed across the open space expecting to feel a hard hand land on her shoulder or a bullet in her back at any moment.

She was actually surprised when she reached the front door. With a grunt, she twisted the knob and pushed inside.

Only to come to a screeching halt when she saw the man sitting in the recliner holding a gun and aiming it at her.

"Hello, Kaylee. Not the person I've been waiting for, but you'll do."

SIXTEEN

"I'm sorry," Walter said. "I'm lost. I know this was the way. But now I'm a little turned around."

Joshua was ready to pull his hair out. He drew in a breath, doing his best to hang on to his rapidly fading patience. "Okay, forget leading us there," Clay said. "Just tell me what to look for and I'm going to tell the chopper."

Walter rubbed a shaky hand over his eyes. He was clearly distressed and if finding Kaylee wasn't so urgent, Joshua would feel sorry for the man. Right now, he just wanted to shake him, rattle his brain a little in the hope of shaking his memories loose.

"Wait a minute. It was remote, pretty high up, but there was a large house about a mile before I got to the cabin. On the right. Like a really big house."

Clay frowned. "The Madisons' home?"

"I don't know the Madisons, but it's got white columns. And it's brick, I think, with a wrought iron fence."

"Sounds like their house. Let's head that way."

Five minutes later, they pulled to a stop in front of the well-lit home. "This is it. I remember this."

"Which way now?" Joshua asked.

Walter pinched the bridge of his nose then pressed shaky fingers to his temples. "Um…"

"Come on, Walter."

"I'm trying, Doc, I really am."

Joshua closed his eyes, once again trying to shut out the vision of Kaylee in Talbot's clutches. "I know, Walter. Just keep trying."

He took a breath. "All right, let's go this way." He pointed. "Around the curve there. It's right around here, I know it is. Maybe."

The chopper buzzed overhead, but Joshua wasn't holding out much hope that they'd spot anything. In spite of Walter saying he recognized a lot of the landmarks, Joshua wondered if he was remembering them from today or sometime in his past. And if it was from the past, then Kaylee didn't stand a chance.

Kaylee didn't move. She almost didn't dare breathe. The man holding the weapon on her stood slowly.

"Why?" she asked. "Just tell me why."

"It really doesn't matter, does it?"

"Of course it does!"

"Because you're a liability—I don't know. I didn't get the whole story. I'm just a hired gun."

Her head pounded in time with her heart. "I don't understand. Did Patrick hire you?"

"Talbot?" He laughed. "Not hardly. Talbot is simply a pawn in this game. But his obsession with you has come in quite handy."

A pawn? "Who's calling the shots then? If this is a chess game, who are the players?" If her heart beat any faster, she was going to pass out. Trying to have a conversation with a killer to buy some time wasn't as easy as it looked in the movies.

The small cabin didn't offer much in the way of cover should the man start shooting. The front door was shut behind her. The small galley kitchen to her right would just trap her. The living area to her left held a couch, a recliner and small flat-screen television. No cover there. Her only option was to get out of the cabin.

The door swung open and Kaylee spun. Patrick. He stopped when he spotted them. His eyes were already turning black and blood covered his face from the broken nose—and probably from his fall. He stood, swaying, staring. Then he blinked before focusing on the other man. "What are you doing here?"

"Cleaning up your mess. What happened to you?"

"I happened to him," Kaylee snapped. "And I'm going to happen to you, too, if someone doesn't tell me where my baby is!"

The man with the weapon raised a brow. "Spunky. No wonder Talbot's so taken with you." He turned the weapon from Kaylee to Patrick. "Too bad it's all got to end now. Watching him chase you has been entertaining to say the least."

Patrick stumbled back against the wall. "What are you talking about, Randy? And what do you mean 'cleaning up my mess'?"

"You're such a lovesick idiot, you can't even see the trail you've left behind. You really think no one is going to come after her? After you? And if someone comes after you, they're going to find me. I can't have than happen."

Patrick raised a hand as though to ward off his words. "We had a deal. You got the baby. I got her."

"Deals are made to be broken. Sorry about this, old friend." He pulled the trigger twice.

Kaylee screamed and dove into the small kitchen

anyway. She landed hard and rolled to her knees next to the cabinet. When she lifted her eyes, they landed on Patrick—now dead on the floor near the door. Silent prayers lifted as her heart pounded in her throat.

"Now, Kaylee," Randy said, "don't be like that. I promise to make it painless and quick." He paused. "Although, I should make you suffer for all the work you've caused me. Killing you has been the most difficult job of my career. So, you can take comfort in that, if you want."

She didn't answer.

His footsteps drew closer. Slow and measured, as though he had all the time in the world. And she supposed he did. Where would she go?

She climbed to her feet and faced him. She wouldn't be shot cowering on the floor. Her eyes met his and he stopped his approach. For a moment, she thought she saw a flash of respect in his hard eyes but then it was gone.

A sound reached her ears. A fast and steady *thump, thump, thump.*

Randy flinched and looked up.

Kaylee threw herself at him with a wild scream. She connected with his chest and he stumbled back to slam against the window.

Glass broke. He yelled and Kaylee shot toward the front door, sidestepping the unmoving Patrick. She threw open the door and staggered down the porch steps.

"Kaylee!" Joshua. He ran toward her, eyes frantic, jaw set. "Get down!"

She heard the crack of the pistol even as she felt Joshua's hand grab her shoulder to yank her down. On the ground, she lay there, stunned, waiting for the pain to come. But nothing did. Had he missed her?

He must have.

And then Clay was there. "You okay?"

"Yes."

"Get to the cruiser and get in the back. Now." He rushed off and she heard him yell, "Police! Stop!"

Thuds and grunts reached her and she rolled to see Joshua and the man who wanted her dead locked together in hand-to-hand combat. The chopper hovered, its spotlight centered on the two men. Her attacker's weapon had fallen from his hand—probably due to a well-placed kick from Joshua.

But her attacker had obviously had some of the same martial arts training that Joshua had because he moved in much the same way, dodging Joshua's kicks and punches. And then the man landed a solid hit to Joshua's head. Joshua flinched and stumbled backward. But when her attacker moved in for another hit, Joshua sidestepped, ducked and threw a counterpunch ending with a spin and a kick to his solar plexus.

The man went to his knees and Joshua caught him in the chin with the heel of his foot. Her attacker went to the ground on his stomach and stayed there.

Joshua backed off, still in a defensive stance. "Kaylee?" he called, never taking his eyes from the man in front of him. "You okay?"

"Yes!"

Clay hurried over, weapon trained on the man. "Be still! Keep your hands where I can see them."

The man Patrick had called "Randy" didn't move. His eyes remained shut. Had Joshua knocked him out with that last kick? The gun was still too close to his hand for her liking, even though he'd dropped it when he'd fallen.

Clay kicked the gun out of reach and settled a knee in his back while reaching for his handcuffs.

Randy's eyes popped open, meeting hers for a split second.

"Clay!" she cried. "Watch out!"

The man bucked, knocking Clay off balance.

Joshua jumped back in with a quick kick that glanced off her attacker's shoulder.

And then Randy was back up on his feet, a knife in his left hand. He slashed at Joshua, who leaped back, then turned for a swipe at Clay, who was just getting his feet under him.

The blade caught Clay across his left bicep. He cried out but lifted his weapon and fired three times center-mass.

Randy finally went down. Dead before he hit the ground. Law enforcement moved in.

Kaylee squeezed her eyes shut and turned away. Backup had arrived with lights flashing and sirens blaring. Better late than never, she supposed. And then Joshua's arms were around her. She didn't even have to look to know who held her.

She shook herself. "Clay." She looked up at Joshua. "I need to check on him."

"He's okay. He waved me over here to you."

She found Clay next to the dead man, cuffing him anyway. A professional to the end, he'd take no chances.

Kaylee hurried over to him. Blood dripped from the wound, but it wasn't pouring. "Are you okay?"

Clay nodded. "I'm fine." He looked up at her as Joshua caught up with her once more.

Kaylee caught her breath on a sob and turned to bury her face against Joshua's shoulder. "What now? How are we going to find Duncan now?"

Because the only man that could have told her his location was now dead.

Clay and the crime scene unit from Nashville were going through the cabin with a fine-tooth comb.

"Looks like Talbot's been staying here for a while," Joshua said.

Clay nodded. "No wonder we couldn't find him." He moved to the desk, favoring his wounded arm.

"You should get that stitched up," Kaylee said.

"I will eventually." He pulled open a drawer and several papers fell to the floor. "What's this?"

Joshua, who had been holding Kaylee while the officers searched, moved to look over Clay's shoulder. "It's a bank statement."

"The address is Talbot's home in Nashville forwarded to this address, but the name on the account is for a Grant Jones."

"Probably a fake name," Joshua said.

"Probably." Clay looked around. "Hey, Logan, do you have the stuff you took off Talbot?"

Logan used a gloved hand to snag a bag from the kitchen counter. "Right here."

"Can you open the wallet and tell me whose name is on the license?"

Logan pulled the wallet from the bag and found the license. "Grant Jones."

Kaylee gasped. "He used a false ID."

"A good one," Clay said. "Talbot didn't do all this alone. And I'm not sure the other guy, Randy Morris, did, either." He pulled his phone from his pocket and dialed a number.

While he talked, Joshua turned to Kaylee. "Are you okay?"

"I'm grateful I'm alive, but so, so worried about Duncan."

He pulled her close and she rested her head on his chest with a deep sigh. Joshua lowered his chin to her head and closed his eyes. "I know. I am, too."

Clay was still talking, so Joshua led Kaylee outside to the porch and they sat on the glider. She snugged up against him. "He really thought he could get away with it."

"He did."

She shook her head. "He would have killed me if I hadn't cooperated with him. I wonder if I could have found a way to escape."

Joshua placed a hand under her chin and lifted her face to his. "Don't go there. It didn't happen. You don't have to wonder about solutions to a problem that doesn't exist."

Her eyes softened and she nodded. "You're right. I need to focus my energy not on the what-ifs, but on finding my son."

"Exactly."

Clay stepped outside to join them. "This cabin is a rental. The owner said Grant Jones signed a six-month lease."

"So, he planned to keep her here," Joshua muttered.

"Yeah. It's secluded. No cell service, no nosy neighbors, just mail service. And who pays attention to that?"

"Right." Clay held a bank statement out to Joshua. "Take a look."

Joshua raised a brow. "There's a ten-thousand-dollar deposit two days after Talbot was released from custody. The account was opened with it."

"Can you trace where it came from?" Kaylee asked.

"I can't, but I know someone who can."

Clay snapped a picture of the statement and emailed it to his contact. "Now, we get Kaylee home, I'll take a statement, and we'll wait to see what shakes loose when CSU finishes processing the place."

Kaylee looked around and shook her head. "He was never here."

"Duncan?" Joshua asked.

She nodded. "There's nothing here to indicate a baby was ever in this cabin. No bottles, diapers, blankets, nothing. He was so convincing." Her voice shook on the last word.

Joshua's heart ached for her. "Yes, but don't blame yourself. He was fully invested in what he was doing and would have said anything to get you to come with him. Including that he had Duncan."

"But he didn't. So, who does?"

SEVENTEEN

Kaylee woke to the sound of dishes clattering and the smell of bacon frying. She sat up and rubbed her eyes then glanced at the still-empty bassinet. Heart aching, she rose and got ready for the day.

Or what was left of it. Her clock said she'd managed a long, if fitful, sleep. She'd been plagued with nightmares of Patrick chasing her with duct tape and a knife, climbing trees and Randy capturing her, only to jump to a faceless woman holding Duncan and laughing that Kaylee would never see him again.

It had been a horrid six hours, and she was ready to wash the dreams away with a hot shower.

Twenty minutes later, she entered the kitchen to find her father sitting at the table with the newspaper spread before him and Clay talking on the phone, demanding someone meet him there.

She looked at her father. "Hi, Dad. What are you doing here?"

"Just came to offer my support. If that's all right. I was frantic when I heard you'd been kidnapped, as well, but I'll leave if you want me to." A flush crept up his throat and into his cheeks. He waited, his eyes not quite meeting hers, and she realized he expected her to shut him out or to ask him to leave. Pain arched through her. She needed her father.

Clasping his fingers, she waited until he finally met her gaze. "No, not at all. Thank you for coming. I want you here."

He started like she'd slapped him. Then his eyes filled. He cleared his throat and looked away. But his fingers tightened on hers for a brief moment.

Clay hung up and her attention was diverted. "Who was that?" she asked. "Meet you where?" The special agents were taking notes and making plans. "What's going on, Clay?"

"We think we know where Duncan is."

A gasp slipped from her and her knees wobbled. She sank into the nearest chair. "Where?"

"With the Rosettis."

Her hope crashed. "You searched there, remember?"

"I remember. But the money transfer came from Robert Morrison's account."

"Who's Robert Morrison?"

"The guy posing as Randy Morris. The one who tried to kidnap you the day Duncan was born."

"Oh. So, why do you think the Rosettis are involved?"

"Because Morrison is employed with White Rose Construction."

She still didn't get it. "Okay. So?"

"So, White Rose Construction is part of the Rosetti empire. The feds think it's a front for some illegal activities going on. It's actually being investigated as we speak."

"So, it all comes back to them, doesn't it?" she said.

"It does."

A knock on the door brought the dogs to their feet,

barking. Clay placed a hand on his weapon and walked to the front. After peering out the window, he opened the door. "Come on in, you're just in time for food."

Joshua stepped inside and came to her side. "Did you get some sleep?"

"Yes. A bit."

"Good."

"Did you hear?" she asked him. "They think Duncan is with the Rosettis."

"Yeah, Clay called and told me. I came as quick as I could. Had to treat a few patients this morning first, though."

"That's fine." She inhaled a deep breath. "I want to go to the Rosettis," she told Clay.

He frowned. "Kaylee—"

"I'm not taking no for an answer. When do we leave?"

He sighed and rubbed his eyes. "As soon as we get a team in place surrounding the house. But, understand, we're just going to do some surveillance first. See if there's any activity that suggests there's a baby in the house."

"Fine," Kaylee said. "That shouldn't take long." She paused. "Tony's family blames me for his death. At least, his parents do. They hate me, but as angry as they were with him, Tony was still blood. And so is Duncan. Maybe I've been stupid," she said softly. "Maybe blood trumps everything."

Joshua's fingers squeezed hers. "Let's not jump to conclusions."

She nodded, but in her heart, she was already jumping.

Joshua was pretty sure time had crept to a stop. It might have even started going backward. Which would be fine if it could take them back to the night Duncan was taken and they could have a do-over.

But since he was pretty sure that wasn't going to be the case, he decided to stop glancing at the time on his phone. He'd driven Kaylee separately from the law enforcement officers, and his SUV was quiet. She'd yet to take her gaze from the house for very long.

On the outside, there was nothing that said, "Kidnapped baby is here."

"I want to go in," she finally said.

"I don't think they want to do that yet."

"I'm not really concerned about what they want. If Duncan is in there, I want to go get him." She huffed. "We're sitting here, twiddling our thumbs, and all I have to do is walk up to the front door and ring the bell."

"What if they don't let you in? What if your presence tips them off?"

She sighed. "The house is surrounded by cops. Where are they going to go? What are they going to do?"

"I don't know, but desperate people do desperate things. I think it's best just to hang tight and see what Clay and the others decide."

For a moment, she didn't respond and Joshua wondered if she was going to ignore him. Then she folded her hands in her lap and closed her eyes. She stayed that way for the next thirty minutes and he figured she might be praying.

Clay rapped on his window, jerking Joshua from his thoughts. He rolled the window down. "What is it?"

"Nothing's happening. We're going to sit here a while longer, but if you two want to head into town to grab a bite to eat, take a break, you should do it."

"No," Kaylee said. Her eyes shot fire at Clay. "I'm

not going anywhere until I know whether my son is in that house or not."

Clay nodded. "All right."

"I've let you all handle this, but I think it's time to start knocking on the front door. Will you clear it with whoever it needs clearing with?"

He sighed. "I don't think that's going to happen, Kaylee."

"You really can't stop me, can you?"

A pause. "Technically, no. Probably not. We're not here to make an arrest or to detain anyone. Yet. So, if you wanted to walk up and ring the bell, I don't suppose anyone would stop you."

With a raised brow, Joshua let his gaze ping back and forth between the two. Kaylee gave a slow nod. "Would you like to come with me?"

"I think Joshua and I would like that."

"Fine. Let's go." She opened the door and stepped out of the SUV.

Johsua followed and Clay walked around to join them on the front lawn. "It's nice. I'm surprised they don't live in a gated area."

"The neighborhood was gated," she murmured. "And there are cameras all over the property. They'll know we're here."

"I'll tell the others to hang back until they hear from me."

He radioed it in while Joshua and Kaylee made their way down the walkway and up the steps to the front door. Four majestic, white columns dwarfed them, two on either side. The porch spanned the length of the house and boasted eight rockers. "They ever use those?" Joshua asked.

"Not whenever I've been here," she said and rang

the doorbell. "Can't exactly picture them as front-porch rocking people."

A minute passed before the door opened and Joshua found himself looking at a woman in her late fifties with salt-and-pepper hair. Her dark green eyes narrowed. "Can I help you?"

"Hello, Isabella."

The woman gasped as she spotted Kaylee. "What are you doing here?"

"I came to get my son."

EIGHTEEN

Kaylee almost regretted her blunt statement when her mother-in-law backpedaled, hand to her chest. Then she blinked and regained her composure. "Get away from here. You're not welcome here."

"This is Joshua Crawford," Kaylee said as though the woman hadn't spoken, "and Sheriff Clay Starke from Wrangler's Corner. Joshua, Clay, this is my former mother-in-law, Isabella Rosetti."

Both men nodded.

"Could we come in for a moment, Mrs. Rosetti?" Kaylee had seldom called the woman anything other than her formal name. And the woman had never asked her to do otherwise.

"No, you certainly may not. I thought we were rid of you."

Kaylee did her best to hide her flinch.

"Who is it, Mama?"

Kaylee stepped to the side so the woman coming down the steps could see her through the open door.

"Kaylee?"

"Hi, Marla."

"Oh, my, what are you doing here? Come in." She reached the bottom of the stairs and walked over to hug

Kaylee. Then she shot a side-glance at her mother as though thinking maybe she shouldn't have been quite so affectionate.

But Isabella was looking up the stairs. Kaylee's gaze followed, but she saw nothing. Kaylee introduced Joshua and Clay again.

"Um...well, come into the den," Marla said.

"She said she's here to get her son," Isabelle said. "You tell her how ridiculous she's being and she needs to go home. I'm going to lie down."

"Please don't go anywhere," Clay said. "We'd really appreciate it if you'd stay and answer some questions."

"No."

"Yes, you will, Mama," Marla said and grasped her mother's right bicep in a firm grip.

The woman wrung her hands. "Well, I suppose."

"Is your husband here?" Clay asked.

"No. He's at work and doesn't need to be bothered with whatever this is." She looked at Kaylee. "Why would you think your son is here? Someone already came looking and found nothing, remember?"

"I remember."

They filed into the living area and took their seats. Joshua and Kaylee on the couch and Clay taking one of the wingback chairs near the fireplace. Mrs. Rosetti sank onto the other one and Marla stood next to her mother, hand on her shoulder. "So, why come back here?"

"Because this is where the trail led us," Clay said. "When Patrick Talbot was released from prison, he started stalking Kaylee again. Over time, due to several different incidents, we came to realize there were two men involved. Last night, Talbot took Kaylee, but she managed to escape and Talbot was killed, but we haven't managed to find her son, yet. We think the man who was helping Talbot was also helping someone else. Someone who wanted the baby alive and Kaylee out of the picture—or dead."

Both women gasped and gaped at Clay.

"Who would do that?" Marla asked.

"We don't know. That's why we're here. Talbot had a connection with a man named Robert Morrison. Robert Morrison had a connection with White Rose Construction, which is owned by your family, Mrs. Rosetti."

The woman's face twitched. "What kind of connection?"

"It looks like someone paid Mr. Morrison a large amount of money, of which he passed a portion to Mr. Talbot. Mr. Talbot and Mr. Morrison are both dead now, but before they died, they indicated someone else was calling the shots."

"And you think it's my husband?"

"Like I said, I think it's someone who wants Kaylee dead, but wants her baby alive." Clay leaned forward and clasped his hands between his knees. "Do you know anyone who might fit that description?"

"Of course not!" Mrs. Rosetti leaped to her feet. "Get out of my house and take your nasty insinuations with you."

"Sit down, Mama." At her daughter's sharp tone, Mrs. Rosetti froze, eyes widening. Then she planted herself back in the chair and clamped her lips together.

Marla drew in a deep breath and turned to face Kaylee. "Now, what makes you think your son is here?"

Kaylee sighed and shook her head. She looked around. Nothing indicated a baby lived here. No bassinet, no blankets, no diapers. Nothing. Just like Misty's home. She rubbed her eyes. "I'm sorry. I think this was a mistake." She stood.

Mrs. Rosetti crossed her arms and narrowed her eyes. "Of course it's a mistake, you stupid woman. I'll never know what Tony saw in you. Get out of my house and don't come back."

Tears gathered. Kaylee knew she shouldn't take the words to heart, but they hurt. A lot. "Yes, I'll do that." She looked at her former sister-in-law. "I'm sorry, Marla."

"I am, too, Kaylee."

Clay and Joshua frowned at her, but stood. "I'm not ready to let this go so easily," Clay said. "I think talking to Mr. Rosetti would be best. When will he be home?"

"Tonight," Marla said.

A low cry reached Kaylee's ears and she froze. She knew that cry. "Duncan?" She followed the sound into the kitchen.

But the room was empty, and the cries had stopped. She frowned, and a cry came from behind her.

Spinning, she spied the monitor on the kitchen counter and raced over to grab it. A video monitor showed a baby lying in a crib, his cries growing stronger. She whirled to face Marla and her mother. Both women stood like statues, matching expressions of fear on their faces. So, that's why Mrs. Rosetti was so nervous.

Marla held out a hand. "I can explain. That's not Duncan."

"Oh, yes, it is." Kaylee remembered Mrs. Rosetti's instinctive glance at the stairs and darted for them. "Duncan!"

"Kaylee! Come back here!" Marla's words bounced off her as she took the stairs two at a time. At the top, she followed the sound of her son's crying and burst into the room at the end of the hall.

For a moment, she could only stare. It was decorated for a baby boy. In detail. The room reflected several weeks' worth of work. Kaylee strode toward the crib and looked down to see her son wailing his little heart out.

"Oh, Duncan." She reached for him and something slammed into her back. The breath flew from her lungs and she went to the floor.

"Marla! Open the door! What are you doing?" Joshua pounced on the door. It shook, but was solid oak. He turned back to Clay, who was speaking into his phone.

Marla's mother stood behind Clay. She spun and ran back down the stairs. Joshua followed her. He didn't know where she was going, but she wasn't getting away. At the bottom of the stairs, she flew down a hall, into a room and slammed the door. He heard the lock click into place.

Duncan's cries came from the kitchen, so he detoured and grabbed the monitor. At least they could see what was happening in the room.

"...going to do?" Kaylee asked. She lay on the floor looking up at Marla, who held a gun on her.

Joshua shuddered. He'd just gotten her back from a madman. No way was he going to lose her now. He raced back to the nursery door and held the monitor so Clay could see it. He frowned when he saw the weapon. "That's not good. How does she think a gun's going to help her out in this situation?"

Clay seemed to be talking to himself so Joshua didn't bother with an answer. "Mrs. Rosetti ran into the bedroom on the ground floor. You need to get someone to cover it."

"On it." Clay passed the word and got confirmation that officers were moving inside the house and looking for the woman.

Both men watched the monitor. "What are we going to do, Clay? We can't bust the door down. Not with her holding a gun on them."

"I know. Let's just watch a minute. Kaylee's talking. Maybe she'll convince her to put the weapon down."

But it didn't look like that was the case to Joshua.

"Pick him up," Marla said.

Kaylee didn't hesitate. She snatched Duncan from the crib and cradled him against her. His cries ceased almost immediately and she turned sideways, putting her body between the gun and the baby. "Marla, there are cops all around this house. Not just Clay, but reinforcements from the Nashville Police Department, the FBI and others. Please, just put the gun down and don't make this any worse."

"Don't make this any worse?" Marla laughed. A sarcastic, incredulous sound that scraped down Joshua's nerves and set his teeth on edge. "I'm not making it worse. I'm going to make it all better."

"How?"

"Because Tony Junior is now the male heir. My father was going to leave everything to Tony, did you know that? In spite of his behavior, his drinking and unacceptable behavior. He was still going to leave it all to him." She waved the gun toward the ceiling before bringing it back to rest on Kaylee.

"Where's backup?" Joshua asked Clay.

"They're here. Waiting for me to give the order to move in, but I can't do that yet."

"No, not with that gun on Kaylee and Duncan."

Joshua turned back to the monitor to hear Kaylee say to Marla, "His name is Duncan."

"Not anymore. Now, we're leaving and you're my hostages. There's no way they'll try to stop me with you holding Duncan. We're going to go down to the garage and get in the Land Rover. Understand? His car seat is in there."

"And then what, Marla? You're going to shoot me and dump my body somewhere?"

"Exactly. Now move."

She was flat-out crazy, Kaylee decided. "Why Duncan? What about your husband? You can have children."

"No, actually, I can't. But even if I could, it wouldn't matter to my father. He's all about his son and carrying on the family name. So, it has to be TJ."

TJ? Tony Junior. Kaylee barely held on to her breakfast. "But your father kicked him out, remember? He disowned him. Which was one of the reasons he felt compelled to marry me."

"Which was stupid and he realized that when Tony was in that bad wreck and almost died. He spend days at the hospital, remember?"

Yes. She did. And she'd hoped it meant reconciliation for father and son. "What about when he was arrested for drugs? I was there at court. Your father was furious. He said he was done with him."

"Yes, Papa does have a raging temper, but it fizzles as quickly as it ignites. He was angry. Just about as angry as I've ever seen him, but Tony was a product of his environment and Papa knew it. He let him stew in a cell for a while then bailed him out."

"No, he didn't. I did. I bailed him out." With practically the last little bit of her savings.

Marla frowned. "Whatever. He went down there and Tony promised to be on his best behavior from then on. At least until the court date. Papa made sure he was taken care of."

"He gave him the money, didn't he?"

"I'm sure."

She was a blind idiot. Kaylee had been played in every way possible. She'd thought she and Tony were struggling to make it on their own—and in her defense, Tony had let her think that. But all along, Tony had been receiving money from his father. She'd thought it was debt. That he'd been using a credit card she didn't know about. "He didn't have to marry me, did he?"

"No. But after that one stunt with the drugs and guns, my father decided he had to take a stand. Tony thought he was serious, that he'd finally pushed our father too far. But Tony got the last laugh. Marrying you made him realize he had to be a little more careful in the future. My father told Tony to get rid of you and he'd give him anything he wanted."

"Get rid of me? Or kill me?"

"Whatever worked."

"So, why kill me? Why want me dead?"

Marla frowned. "No one wanted you dead. I just wanted your baby."

Now Kaylee was confused. "Someone tried to kidnap me the day Duncan was born. Someone shot at us coming out of the hospital. And the bullets came really close to Duncan. And, again, someone attacked me in the doctor's office in Wrangler's Corner. How can you say no one wanted me dead?"

Marla huffed. "I don't know what you're talking about. Let's go."

No, something wasn't adding up. She was missing something. But what?

"Go! Now!"

Kaylee started for the door only to have Marla stop her. "Not that one." She pointed. "That one."

The closet?

She walked toward it, cradling Duncan. She paused. "I need a bottle for him. He's going to be fussy soon."

"I'm not stupid, you know." Marla walked to a cabinet and opened a door, revealing shelves full of formula. "Get some and put it in the baby bag."

Kaylee did as ordered. "How did you know about the door? That it wasn't armed with an alarm?"

"Easy. I was there that day, you know? When you moved in? I was going to use the cover of all the commotion to grab TJ, but that woman wouldn't move away from him. When I realized I wasn't going to get him alone, I simply studied your alarm system. It didn't take long to figure it out. When people started leaving, I simply walked into the area to wait."

Kaylee dropped another can of formula into the bag.

"Now, that's it. Anything else, your majesty?" Marla asked, her sarcasm dripping.

Yes, Kaylee wanted to shout. Where were Clay and Joshua? Why hadn't anyone stopped this yet?

Because she held Duncan and a madwoman held a gun on them. No one was going to do anything to jeopardize them. They were waiting, she realized. Waiting for an opening, a chance. Some kind of opportunity to step in and rescue them. And it was up to Kaylee to give them that.

NINETEEN

Joshua tensed as Kaylee walked toward the closet door. "Where's she going? That might not be a closet. Not if she's being instructed to go through it."

"Yeah. That could be a problem."

"We can't let them go through that door. We don't know where it leads."

"I'm thinking."

"Wait, what's she doing?" Joshua pointed. "She's putting Duncan back in the crib."

Kaylee turned to a screeching Marla. "What are you doing? Pick him up and go!"

"I'm not going with you." She walked away from the crib, away from the door where Clay and Joshua stood, and put her back against the wall.

"Get over here or I'll shoot you!"

"Maybe you will, but I'm not letting you use me as a hostage."

Marla stilled. Then nodded. "You're right. I don't need you. Not as long as I have the baby."

"She's going to shoot her," Joshua said. He stood back, lifted a foot and slammed it against the door in a kick that ripped the top hinge from the wall. He spun and landed another kick that sent the door inward.

Marla fired a shot that sent him diving to the floor then rolling to his feet. She took aim and then stumbled to her knees. A fisted hand landed next to her right ear and she screamed.

Another hard punch from Kaylee sent her to the floor where she scrambled, trying to grasp the gun only inches from her fingers.

Clay stepped on Marla's reaching hand and then had a knee in her back, ordering her to be still. In seconds, he had her cuffed.

Kaylee sank to the floor, breathing hard and holding the hand she'd used to punch Marla.

Marla cried, sobs racking her thin frame. "He promised me I could have the baby. He promised me."

"Who?" Clay growled.

"Tony. He promised me if I would just be patient, he'd give me the baby. He was mine!" Spittle flew from her lips as she glared at Kaylee. "Mine. He was never meant to be yours." She lowered her head and sobs took over.

Joshua moved to Kaylee and helped her to her feet while Clay hauled the hysterical woman off the floor and toward the door. "I've got officers on the room where Mrs. Rosetti disappeared. After I put this one in the cruiser, I'll deal with her. You two come when you're ready."

"Thanks." Joshua pulled Kaylee to him and pressed a kiss to her forehead. Then a light one on her lips. "Let's get Duncan and go home."

"Not so fast."

Joshua spun—automatically shoving Kaylee behind him at the threat he heard in the three words—and came face-to-face with Isabella Rosetti who'd slipped into the room via the door Marla had ordered Kaylee to use only moments before. Mrs. Rosetti held her weapon steady and met his gaze with her dark, hard eyes. "Move. Or die."

"I'm not moving," Joshua said. Chilled, he noticed the suppressor on the end. If she fired, no one would hear.

She pulled the trigger and the bullet grazed his arm. He shouted at the burn, yanked a screaming Kaylee to the floor then rolled on top of her. "What are you doing?"

"She has to die."

Duncan yelled his displeasure from his crib.

Kaylee shoved Joshua from her and rolled to her feet. "Why! Just tell me why!"

Duncan still screamed.

"Because you know."

"Know what?"

"About Tony."

Kaylee froze. What did she know? What could she possibly know about Tony that would cause his mother to want her dead? And then it hit her.

"The blood," she whispered. "I corrected you when you told the nurse his blood type."

"Yes."

"Tony isn't your husband's son."

"He is not and my husband can never find out. Do you know what he would do to me?"

She knew. "Kill you."

"My body would never be found. And you are the only one who knew."

"You set this all up. Every last thing, didn't you?" Joshua asked. "You hired that guy to try to kidnap Kaylee the day Duncan was born."

"Yes. I knew of Robert's past and his love of money. He was only too happy to help me."

"But you didn't want Duncan dead, so why…" Kaylee swayed. "You were going let me give birth then kill me."

The woman's cold eyes swung to Joshua. "Unfortunately, things did go quite so easy."

"So, being pregnant is probably the only reason I'm alive right now," Kaylee whispered.

"That's one way to look at it, I suppose. I loved Tony more than life itself. When he died, I wanted to follow him into the grave, but then I learned you were pregnant and his son was my reason to keep going."

Joshua grunted. "You knew about her stalker—everyone knew about it since it was plastered all over the news. You knew about Talbot's release and concocted your plan so you could pin the whole thing on him, didn't you? What about your husband? What's his role in all of this."

"My husband?" She laughed. The sound grating, bordering on the edge of hysteria. "He cares nothing about what I do as long as it doesn't interfere with his world. So, now you know." She lifted the weapon. "Now you can die."

Before Kaylee or Josh could move, Clay appeared and used the grip of his gun against the woman's head. Her eyes rolled back and she slumped to the floor, the weapon clattering harmlessly beside her.

Clay bent over and picked it up then holstered the weapon he'd used to knock Isabella out. "You two are grounded until you can figure out how to keep from attracting people who want you dead." He hauled the unconscious woman from the room with the help of Special Agent James.

Kaylee turned and buried her face in Joshua's uninjured shoulder. Then drew in a deep breath. "I need to feed my child. Then let's get you to the hospital and get that wound looked at."

"Sounds like a good idea to me. Can I just tell you one thing before go?"

She went to the crib and picked up her son. He settled against her and stuffed a fist into his mouth. She turned to find Joshua standing next to her, dripping blood onto the floor. "Of course, but you need to make it quick. We really need to get that arm looked at."

"It's a scratch. But since you want me to make it quick, how's this? Before anyone else comes in and tries to kill us, I have something I need to say."

"Okay. What?"

"I love you."

Kaylee blinked, her breath catching somewhere in the vicinity of her throat. "Oh."

"That's all you have to say?"

"No." Joy exploded through her, but words were hard to get past her lips without adding tears.

He waited. Then cleared his throat. "You want to fill me in on what you're thinking?"

"That *was* fast."

"Oh."

"But I love you, too."

He nearly wilted as he pulled her to him and placed a kiss on her lips, then one on Duncan's red face. "Good. Now that we got that out of the way, please give that child a bottle."

Kaylee grinned and quickly fixed a bottle with the items from the diaper bag.

Joshua took him from her and popped the nipple in the baby's mouth. Silence descended and he led her out of the house.

Kaylee shook her head. She never did anything the

easy way. And sometimes she did things all wrong. She slid a glance at the man beside her. But when she did it right, she *really* did it right.

Two Months Later

Kaylee held her son and watched her father standing at the end of the aisle and pulling on his collar. He'd finally told her why her mother had left. She'd known she was dying and hadn't wanted Kaylee to watch it happen. When her father had said he was too late, he'd simply meant he was too late to have another start with her mother. But he wasn't too late to apologize. And then he'd come home to a daughter who was an exact replica of the woman he'd lost. He'd confessed that every time he'd looked at Kaylee, the guilt consumed him. But he'd never stopped loving her.

Kaylee sighed. Now that they'd cleared the air, they were well on their way to a restored relationship and she couldn't be happier.

Joshua slid in beside her on the pew. "I can't believe they were willing to push the wedding back to now," he whispered.

"Your mother wanted you here."

"I know. And she wanted your help with the planning."

When their parents realized how close they'd come to losing their children and grandchild, they'd been understandably horrified. They'd agreed to wait until all of the legal mess had been taken care of before tying the knot.

And today was the day.

It was a small ceremony, with only about twenty close friends and family. Joshua had offered to give his mother away, but she'd said she'd give herself away and he was to watch everything from a front row seat.

The minister cleared his throat and the ceremony began.

Before she knew it, Kaylee heard, "I now pronounce you man and wife. You may kiss the bride."

Joshua leaned over and covered her lips with his. Kaylee could only smile. When he lifted his head, he whispered, "I wish that was us."

Tears misted her eyes. "Me, too."

"Soon?" he said.

"Soon."

Happiness exploded within her when he took a restless Duncan from her. He settled the baby in the crook of his arm and Duncan slid his three favorite fingers into his mouth. His eyes drooped and he dropped off.

"Walk with me?" Joshua asked her.

"Sure. But what about the reception?"

"We won't be long, but I want to go down to the lake. It's a gorgeous day. Let's take advantage of it."

She smiled. "Okay."

They made their way out of the small country church and Joshua took her hand. "I love this place," he said.

"What? You don't miss Nashville?"

He shook his head. "You know I don't."

She bit her lip. "Are you sure? Because I'll go there with you if it means you'll be happy. Dad paid off your student loans so you don't have to have that hanging over your head."

"I know."

"Are you sure you're all right with that?"

"I'm sure. My mother could have paid them off. She volunteered a few times and I told her no."

"So, why let my dad do it?"

"Because I think he needed to. Not really for me, but for him. To prove something to himself."

Kaylee nodded. "I think you're right. I thought you'd be mad at him."

"I was a little at first, but then—" he shrugged "—the heart behind the gesture was what mattered."

"I'm glad you saw that." She paused. "So, you're happy here? In Wrangler's Corner?"

He walked her out onto the dock that bobbed gently beneath them. "I'm happy, Kaylee, and it doesn't have one thing to do with a place. I'm happy because I'm with you and Duncan."

"You're going to make me cry, aren't you?"

He gave a small laugh then placed a sweet kiss on her lips. "I really love you, Kaylee. Even more than on the day I told you so in a killer's house."

She rolled her eyes. "Will you stop with that already? I was just glad to hear those words come out of your mouth. I didn't care where you said them."

He smiled. "I know. But I want to get this right. Because you deserve it."

"What?"

Carefully balancing Duncan in his left arm, Joshua knelt in front of her and pulled a ring from his pocket with his right hand.

Kaylee sucked in a breath.

"You said soon," he said.

"I did," she whispered.

"Kaylee, will you marry me?"

"Yes." She added a nod to the word just in case it was too strangled for him to understand it.

A grin lightened his face. "Good. Now, can you hold your hand out for me? I'd take it, but I've kind of got an armful here and I don't want to drop the ring."

Laughter escaped her as she held her left hand out to him. He slid the ring on and she stared at it. "It's gorgeous. Amazing, actually. It looks a lot like…" She stopped and held up her hand. The lump in her throat grew bigger. "It's hers, isn't it?"

"Is it all right? I asked your dad and he thought you'd want to wear it, but if not, we can go shopping and—"

She pulled him to his feet, then grasped his head and lowered it until his lips covered hers. She kissed him. Deeply. With as much emotion as she could put into it. When she drew back, she sucked in a lungful of air and did her best to stop the tears. "I would love to wear my mother's ring. I think she would be honored. As I am."

"That's what your dad said."

She smiled through her tears. "I love you, Joshua Crawford."

"And I love you, Kaylee soon-to-be-Crawford." He gave her another kiss then tugged on her hand. "Let's go congratulate the happy couple."

"Let's not say anything about our engagement until later. I don't want to take anything away from them."

"Okay."

They made their way back to the church and Kaylee sent up a silent prayer of thanks to God who'd brought good from tragedy. Who'd brought her home to find love and reconciliation.

Her father hugged her and her stepmother/soon-to-be-mother-in-law kissed her cheek. "He asked, didn't he?"

Kaylee gasped then grinned. "Yes."

"Congratulations, my dear. I'm so very pleased."

"Thank you." She shot a glance at her father then back to Olivia. "So am I. Thank you for being patient with me. And so very kind."

Olivia gave her another tight hug. "I've always

wanted a daughter. I'm glad I get you as a daughter-in-law."

Then they were swarmed with well-wishers until Joshua managed to pull Kaylee outside. "Whew."

"Yeah. No kidding."

He took her hand and walked her to the car. Duncan squirmed and began to fuss. Kaylee reached for him, but Joshua shook his head. "I've got this. He belongs to me, too, right?"

Within seconds, he had a bottle in the little guy's mouth.

Kaylee's heart trembled. "Right. And I'm so glad you belong to me."

Forever and ever.

* * * * *

If you enjoyed this story, look for other books in the WRANGLER'S CORNER *series:*

The Lawman Returns
Rodeo Rescuer
Protecting Her Daughter
Classified Christmas Mission
Christmas Ranch Rescue

Dear Reader,

Thank you for journeying back to Wrangler's Corner for yet another adventure. I hope you enjoyed Joshua's and Kaylee's story. I really loved getting to know them and little Duncan.

You know, Kaylee had a rough time after losing her mother. She had questions that had never been answered because of her estrangement from her father. She didn't really think people could change and was really reluctant to give him a second chance. And while it's true, some people really don't change, others really do. I was glad to make Kaylee's father one of those who did. And when Kaylee finally stopped judging him and decided to give him another chance, she was so glad she did. Sure, she was risking being hurt all over again, but in the end, she found it worth the risk. And sometimes that's what life is all about. Taking risks—that step of faith that allows God to step in and do something good.

Blessings to all and I look forward to having you join me soon on another adventure in Wrangler's Corner.

God bless,
Lynette Eason

Get 4 FREE REWARDS!

We'll send you 2 FREE Books plus 2 FREE Mystery Gifts.

Love Inspired® Suspense books feature Christian characters facing challenges to their faith... and lives.

FREE Value Over $20

SPECIAL EXCERPT FROM

Love Inspired
SUSPENSE

*When Chase McLear is accused of aiding the Red Rose
Killer, can Maisy Lockwood, the daughter of one of
the victims, help him clear his name before they both
become targets?*

Read on for a sneak preview of
STANDING FAST by **Maggie K. Black***,*
the next book in the **MILITARY K-9 UNIT** *miniseries,*
available July 2018 from Love Inspired Suspense!

The scream was high-pitched and terrified, sending
Senior Airman Chase McLear shooting straight out of
bed like a bullet from a gun. Furious howls from his K-9
beagle, Queenie, sounded the alarm that danger was near.
Chase's long legs propelled him across the floor. He felt
the muscles in his arms tense for an unknown battle, as the
faces of the brave men and women who'd been viciously
killed by Boyd Sullivan, the notorious Red Rose Killer,
flickered like a slide show through his mind.

Sudden pain shot through his sole as his bare foot
landed hard on one of the wooden building blocks his
daughter, Allie, had left scattered across the floor. He
grabbed the door frame and blinked hard. His three-year-
old daughter was crying out in her sleep from her bedroom
down the hall.

Seemed they were both having nightmares tonight.

He started down the hall toward her, ignoring the stinging pain in his foot.

"No!" His daughter's tiny panicked voice filled the darkened air.

"It's okay, Allie! Everything's going to be okay. Daddy's coming!" He reached her room. There in the gentle glow of a night-light was his daughter's tiny form tossing and turning on top of her blankets. Her eyes were still scrunched tightly in sleep.

A loud crack outside yanked his attention to the window at his right. He leaped to his feet and started for the glass just in time to see the blur of a figure rush away through the bushes. His heart pounded like a war drum in his rib cage as he threw open the window. The screen had been slit with what looked like a knife and peeled back, as if someone had tried to get inside

He closed the window firmly, locking it in place. Then he looked down at Queenie. "Stay here. Protect Allie."

Inspirational Romance to Warm Your Heart and Soul

Join our social communities to connect with other readers who share your love!

Sign up for the Love Inspired newsletter at **www.LoveInspired.com** to be the first to find out about upcoming titles, special promotions and exclusive content.

CONNECT WITH US AT:

Harlequin.com/Community

 Facebook.com/LoveInspiredBooks

 Twitter.com/LoveInspiredBks

LISOCIAL2017